TRAVELLER TO
THE EAST

Thomas Mofolo

Translated by Harry Ashton

PENGUIN BOOKS

PENGUIN BOOKS

Published by the Penguin Group
Penguin Books Ltd, 80 Strand, London WC2R 0RL, England
Penguin Group (USA) Inc, 375 Hudson Street, New York, New York 10014,
USA
Penguin Group (Canada), 90 Eglinton Avenue East, Suite 700, Toronto,
Ontario, Canada M4P 2Y3 (a division of Pearson Penguin Canada Inc)
Penguin Ireland, 25 St Stephen's Green, Dublin 2, Ireland (a division of
Penguin Books Ltd)
Penguin Group (Australia), 250 Camberwell Road, Camberwell, Victoria 3124,
Australia (a division of Pearson Australia Group Pty Ltd)
Penguin Books India Pvt Ltd, 11 Community Centre, Panchsheel Park,
New Delhi – 110 017, India
Penguin Group (NZ), Cnr Rosedale and Airborne Roads, Albany, Auckland
1310, New Zealand (a division of Pearson New Zealand Ltd)
Penguin Books (South Africa) (Pty) Ltd, 24 Sturdee Avenue, Rosebank,
Johannesburg 2196, South Africa

Penguin Books (South Africa) (Pty) Ltd, Registered Offices:
24 Sturdee Avenue, Rosebank, Johannesburg 2196, South Africa

www.penguinbooks.co.za

First published by the Morija Sesuto Book Depot, 1907
This translation published by the Society for Promoting Christian
Knowledge, London, 1934
This edition published by Penguin Books (South Africa) (Pty) Ltd 2007

ISBN 978-0-143-18551-2

Typeset by CJH Design in 10 on 12.5 pt Palatino
Cover design: African Icons
Printed and bound by Interpak Books, Pietermaritzburg

Contents

Thomas Mofolo at the time of his first novel
(Courtesy of Morija Museum and Archives, Lesotho)

Autobiographical Sketch

Dear Mr Franz,

You ask me for personal details up to the present.

I was born at Khojane, in the region of Mafeteng, in the month of August, 1877. My day of birth is not known. I was baptised in the Church of Fora (Paris Evangelical Missionary Society) by Moruti Hermann Dieterlen, who is still in France. I entered the Bible School in 1894; in the month of June, 1896, I entered the Mountain School at Morija and in December of that year I passed my First Year Examination. In 1897 I passed the Second Year and the School Elementary. On account of the rinderpest I lacked money for school fees and wrote and told Mr Dyke that I was not coming back to school in 1898. During that week I went to the Maloti to bring down horses to take me to work among the White people. At dawn I set out to go to work, but when I passed the post office I found a letter from Mr Dyke preventing my going and he ordered me back to school, permitting me to complete my studies 'on credit'.

I turned back at once and went home to tell my parents of the change in plans. In 1898 I passed my Third Year and Moruti Casalis asked me, while I had still a few months in training, to come to help him in the Book Depot after I had passed my examination.

I worked there till the end of 1899. In the beginning of 1900 our work ceased, together with the printing works, on account of the War. I went to Leloaleng Mills to learn how to do carpentry and was a teacher there for two years. In 1902 I left and became a teacher at Bensonvale Institution. As soon as I arrived Mr Dyke called me back to Lesotho and appointed me at Maseru. I was a teacher there till the time of peace, when Mr Casalis engaged me again in the Book Depot, where I wrote my first novel.

I left in 1910 and went to Lealui, whither I was drawn by the high wages, but I had to return on account of illness. Then I went to the Rand where I was engaged in piece work.

Mr Taberer sent me back to Lesotho in 1912 to be labour agent for the Eckstein Group of Mines. I returned to Lesotho with little love for that work, but later I became accustomed to it and actually liked it. In 1922 I even became an independent labour agent, that is, I freed myself from the contract with the Eckstein Group and became an Independent Labour Agent with the right to recruit for whomsoever I wanted. I recruited for Mr Taberer and for the Rand Mines, for the Diamond Mines, Sugar Plantations in Natal, Collieries, Farm-work, etc, etc.

By November, 1925, I had opened a branch of my business here in Teyateyaneng, and put my brother, Ben Mofolo, in charge. In 1927 he resigned, and so I left the recruiting business in 1928. I forgot to tell you that in 1916 I bought a Government Portable Steam Engine and Milling Plant, and so I opened a mill at Ty. This I have now also sold, together with the motor cars attached to the business ...

(Reproduced in G H Franz, 'The Literature of Lesotho', *Bantu Studies*, University of the Witwatersrand Press, September 1930)

Leselinyana
LA
LE-SOTHO
Ea bohlale o ithuta kamehla.

THEKO EA LESELINYANA
KE 6/., KA SELEMO,
KAPA 6 D. KA KHOELI.
LE LEFSHOA QALONG EA SELEMO.
SESUTO BOOK DEPOT, MORIJA, BASUTOLAND.

LITSEBISO TSA LIPEHI
LI LEFSHOA 2/6, LEHA E LE TSA
MANYALO.
LIPATLO TSE LING LE LITSEBISO
LI JA 2/6 KA INCH.

SELEMO SA 40   No 1   1 PHEREKHONG, 1907

MOETI OA BOCHABELA

LEFIFING le letšo, le reng tšo, mehleng ea ha lichaba li sa ntsane li jana joaleka libatana tsa naha, motho o na a le teng ea bitsoang Fekise. E, ke re motho e seng motho sebopeho, le ho tseba ho bua feela; empa motho lipuong, motho liketsong, motho mekhoeng eohle; motho sephiring le pontšeng, motho bohlokong le thabong, boiketlong le bothateng, tlaleng le naleng.

Kamehla sebopeho sa hae se seng, ha a na se seng. Seo u 'monang a le sona kajeno, ke seo a leng sona kamehla. Ngoana oa setsoha-lepelo-ea-maobane, kamoo ba-Sotho ba bolelang kateng.

E ne e le motho ka botlalo bohle ba lentsoe lena le reng "MOTHO", motho kamoo 'Mopi a neng a rere hore motho a be joalo, setšoantšo

sa sebele sa Ea entseng tsohle tse bonoang le tse sa bonoeng, eo ho nong ho lekangoa eena ea joalo ha ho thoe tsohle libopuoa tse ling li tla mo tšaba, li tla mo utloa, li mo hlonephe kahobane o na le khanya e 'ngoe e sele, eo libopuoa tse ling li se nang eona.

Litaba tsa motho eo re 'molelang, re itše ke tsa khale, tsa boholo-holo mehleng ea ha lefatše lena la Africa le ne le sa aparetsoe ke lefifi le leholo, lefifi le tšabehang, leo tsohle tsa lefifi li etsoang ka lona. Ke tsa mehleng ea ha ho no ho se borena ho tiileng, lichaba li sa hlola li jana. E sa re motho ha a robala, a robale ka letsoalo la hore lira li se ke tsa mo oela hoimo, a sa ile le boroko. Hobane ba bangata ba ne ba robala e le khotso, ho sa bonahale letho feela la lira; ere ha motho a robetse, a tsosoe ke lerumo feela, lira li se li fihlile; kapa a tsosoe ke mollo, ntlo eo a leng ho eona e se e e-cha; kapa a tsosoe ke mokhosi le ke lerata. Monna a tatamale, a siee mosali le bana, Mosali a tatamale a siee monna le bana, a

ba hopole a se a le hole. Ngoana a tsohe a sa bone ntat'ae, a se a sa bone le a mong oa bao a ba tsebang, a se a bona batho ba sele ba tiileng ho patela ha babo. Hangata, motho o na robala le bana ba hae e le khotso, e le nala, 'me ere ha bo e-sa, monna a be a le koo! Mosali a le koo!... 'Me e be ke karohano ke ho fela. Monna o tla batla bana ba hae a be a ba tele. Le mosali joalo. A karohano e bohloko!... Batho ba sa aroha'ngoa ke lefu.

Lichaba li ne li jana, li tsoelane lipelo, li tšoana le liphoofolo tsa naha.

Mehleng eo, mona o no o jele setai haholo. Ba nang le lintho ke bona ba neng ba pateloa ka sehlohoso ere tsoa se bolela. Matla e ne e le tokelo mehleng eo. 'Mampoli, tokelo tsohle e ne e le tsa hae, a etsa kamoo a ratang kateng. 'Nete e ne e sa tsejoe lefatšeng, e ne e oeloa. Ho bolaea, e ne e se ntho e makalloang haholo. Leshano ne e ne e le eona 'nete, 'nete e le leshano. Ho utsoa, mahlong a ba

bangata, e ne e se ho utsoa, e ne e le ho iphelisa. Sebe sa nama e ne e se sebe, e ne e le sebe feela ha motho a tšoeroe. Morena oa secha-ba o na a etsa ka batho ba hae kamoo a ratang kateng: a bolaea bao a ba hloileng kantle ho moluto, kapa a ba tlatlapa lintho tsa bona. Ho no ho se motho ea lulang a ikethe ha hae, batho ba ne ba lula ka matsoalo joaleka matsa.

Motho eo re bolelang tsa hae o phetse mehleng ea ha lefatše la Africa le sa ntsane le tebile hakalo, le sa le botšong ruri.

T. M.

(Li sa tla)

THOMASE MOFOLO

Sketches of Thomas Mofolo, and of the Morija mission station with the printshop where he worked on the left, made by Frédéric Christol for the *Golden Book*, published in Paris in 1912

The frontispiece by Walter Battiss used in several translated editions of John Bunyan's *The Pilgrim's Progress*, with the adventurous African traveller setting off

1

The Darkness of Old

In the black darkness, very black, in the times when the tribes were still eating each other like wild beasts, there lived a man called Fekisi.

Yes, I say a man, not a man in appearance only, one knowing how to speak, but a man in speech, in actions, in all his habits; a man in secret and openly; a man in grief and joy; in good fortune and bad; in hunger and plenty.

His nature was always the same, he did not alter. As you saw him today, so you would see him always, he was the child of one who 'gets up with the same heart as yesterday,' as the Basuto say.

He was a man in the full meaning of the word 'man', a man as the Creator planned man to be, a true image of Him who made all things visible and invisible, the very man described when it was said: All creatures shall fear him, shall be obedient to him and shall honour him, because he has a glory of his own, which other creatures do not possess.

The story of this man of whom we speak, we have said, is of old times, when this land of Africa was still clothed in great darkness, dreadful darkness, in which all the works of darkness were done. It is of the days when there was no strong chieftainship, the tribes still ate each other. So when a person went to sleep, he did so in terror that his enemies might fall upon him in his sleep. For many a man would go to sleep in peace, without the smallest sign of any enemy, and when he was asleep, he would be wakened up by a spear, with his enemies already upon him. Or he would be wakened by fire to find his hut already in flames, or he might be awakened by an alarm and disturbance. The husband would run away, leaving wife and children, the wife would run away leaving husband and children, remembering them when she was far away. A child would wake up and would not see his father or one of those whom he knew, but only strangers who had come to surprise his village. Often a man would go to sleep with his children in peace and plenty, and when day dawned, the man was far away, the woman was far away, and that was a separation, the end of everything. The man would look for his children, and his wife also, until he gave up in despair. A painful separation. It is not death which separates these people.

The tribes ate each other, they hated each other, they were as animals.

In those days jealousy had increased very much. Those who had possessions were attacked with that cruelty we have just spoken about. Might was right in those days. All the rights belonged to the strong man, he did as he wished. Truth was not known on the earth, it was met but rarely. To kill was not a thing which caused much astonishment. A lie was the truth, truth was a lie. To steal, in the eyes of many, was not to steal, but a means of livelihood. A sin of the flesh was no sin, it was a sin only when the person was caught. The chief of a tribe treated his people as he wished; he killed for no fault those whom he hated, or he robbed them of their goods. There was no man who lived happily in his home, people lived in fear like buck.

The person whose history we are telling lived in the days when the land of Africa was still sunk in this low state, still truly in darkness.

The origin of the Basuto appears not to be too well known.

When our elders speak of themselves they say, the tribe of the Basuto comes from Ntsoanatsatsi. But no one knows where that Ntsoanatsatsi is, or in what country. Basuto of old, even those who lived then, truly believed that there is a living God, who has made all things. They agreed that God rejects all evil things. They would say, God hates witchcraft and such things. When the Basuto lost a person through death, they placed by his body seeds of various kinds, and said to the dead man, 'Oho! Sleep for us! Ask for rain for us! Give us Kaffir-corn, pumpkins!' and so on.

By speaking thus, they made as if he who was dead, although he was dead, still heard them. At the burial there was lamentation, songs which indeed saddened the heart were sung. This is one of them:

We have been left outside,
We have been left lamenting,
We have been left in sorrow.
Oh, if I also could be taken to heaven!
Why am I without wings, that I might take myself there!
If there were but a rope hanging down,
Which I would seize upon
And ascend to my friends in happiness!

Such songs show clearly that, even in such darkness, a little knowledge of God was already there: a knowledge that death is not the end of a person was there, because when they took him on his road they spoke to him and certainly thought he heard them.

Our friend was born when matters were so. But he accepted many things which others did not accept, and was very unhappy in his soul. We shall relate briefly what things made him unhappy, and what gave him joy.

2

Fekisi the Kind

Fekisi was a person living, like all Basuto, by ploughing to get his food and that of his parents.

His father was a person of great virtue, so that he milked for his children the milk they drank, that perchance they might resemble him and become people like him. He tried to lead a beautiful life, honourable in the eyes of his people. His mother was a woman who brewed much beer, one who listened much to her husband, who humbled herself in an astonishing fashion when her husband was angry.

Nearby the home of Fekisi was another house, that of Phakoane. Phakoane was a human being when he did not drink; but when he had taken drink, he was as a wild animal. He would curse horribly, fight and make a dreadful noise. He used to go to beer drinks, and on his return would throw himself on people in anger. One day he came in shockingly drunk. On his way home he got lost in the darkness and fell into some ditches. He arrived home red with blood. When he arrived and went to his hut, he found his wife had gone to bed, so he opened the door, closed it and fastened it, he stripped off his blankets, took a stick and beat his wife cruelly. When he stopped beating her, that poor woman was all tired by the stick, so that she was even unable to put on her clothes. There was no fault in that woman. Phakoane, on account of his drunkenness, was quarrelling with her as to the reason she had gone to bed like a lady, when he, her husband, had fallen into ditches. Said the woman: 'I did not know you had fallen.' 'Why did you not know? I say, although I suffer such things, it is you who are always wishing me dead, so that you may remain and be married by others.'

Such is drunkenness, it gives bad things to eat, its fruits are bitter; and when a person is sober, he is sorry when he hears and sees what he has done.

The life at Phakoane's caused Fekisi much grief. He could not understand why Phakoane got married, when here he was making his wife unhappy and always beating her. He asked himself, he said: Now as Phakoane has beaten his wife so much yesterday, beaten her for no reason, now today when he is sober, how does he feel? How will he speak to the woman? What will he say? Will he say why he was quarrelling with her? Will he perhaps continue to go to beer drinks? Or if he does go, will perhaps he not stop drinking when he feels he has had enough, and go home?

But nevertheless, whenever Phakoane heard there was beer at So-and-So's, he stood up briskly. You must understand it was not Phakoane alone who was a drunkard, the whole nation was the same; men and women, all flocked to beer drinks. The men were drunk as well as the women. There were gatherings at the feasts of the schools for boys and girls at dances and such like. A Mosuto drinks till he is full up to the throat, and finally he vomits. When they are drunk like this you will hear some prostitute say: 'Hela! So-and-So or father of So-and-So, won't you see me home, I am so drunk?'

This seeing one another home often led to the birth of young Polos and Makhokolotsos.[1] Moreover with such drunkenness, and at such feasts, quarrels and fights arose, ending in people

---

[1] Names given to illegitimate children.

being killed.

Fekisi was much disturbed in his mind over such happenings. He would wonder why these people drank beer, when it made them do such bad things. A man got up in the morning fit and well, but on account of drunkenness he would return home in the evening all wounds or he might be for ever dead. Perhaps he might be killed in these fights, perhaps he might fall over a precipice through drunkenness and die.

Fekisi's heart was much troubled over the life at Phakoane's, as he lived next to him, but his heart was more troubled by the sight of the whole nation travelling by this same path, the end of which they knew.

He was worried much over those children who were picked up on the paths.[2] He could not understand where love is now. He could not understand what use there was in marriage when a person can leave what is his, and go to what belongs to another. He would ask himself, if matters are like this, in what way is a human being superior to an animal? He would say, an animal is clean and fit for the purpose for which it has been created.

When Fekisi heard the news that there was a feast at a certain place his heart became sore; he would think of the fights and murders which would take place there through drunkenness; he would think of those who would arrive home with broken limbs, or those who would fall dead on the road; he would think of those women also who did not go to beer drinks, who would be ill-treated[3] for no reason, like the wife of Phakoane. All these things were very heavy on his mind, they worried him much.

A third matter which troubled him was the lack of truth

---

[2] That is, illegitimate.
[3] Literally 'killed'.

among the people. Many people invariably lie, they begin to lie even when they are not in trouble. By saying this I mean that when you speak to a person, and ask him something, he tells you something different which he invents, he leaves alone what you ask him about. If a person is in trouble, then we say nothing about it, as it is said we are getting ourselves out of trouble.

He could not understand the reason which made people speak about something which they had not heard or which they had not seen, while a thing which they had seen or heard or which they had done, that they would hide. That which they should tell they hide; they tell what they are not asked.

Even today the temptation to tell a lie instead of the truth is still great, it is still strong among the nation. Again the lie which is painful above all others is that of slander; to say that So-and-So has done such and such a thing, and to say so falsely, to give false evidence. This temptation still prevails today among the nation.

In his youth, we may say, in his boyhood, Fekisi was a herdboy. Herding in Basutoland long ago was bad and painful, so that we may be glad we were born in these times of light.

The herdboys in those days were not boys as they are today. Light-hearted and careless young men used to herd, and fights took place every day. The cattle of the principal herdboy would feed in the pleasant part of the country, in the largest pasture where there was much grass. They grazed long grass alone. At the drinking place the cattle of the principal herdboy were the first to drink when the water was still clean. Above all that, the principal herdboy would bully the others. The boys had to share everything with him when herding, whether bread or meat. He that did not share went herding knowing well that he would get the stick. If the principal herdboy smoked tobacco he forced the boys to get tobacco for him or to steal it from their fathers and bring it to him. If they did not there was more stick.

Fekisi refused to do all these things of which we have just spoken. He would say, each should graze where he wished, water his cattle at any time he liked; they should not wait for anyone who was said to be the chief herdboy and who must water his cattle first.

Fekisi was not a person who liked to fight. But when he was attacked, he fought with astonishing courage and strength. And did he not know how to use a stick! He would fight, but when those who attacked him ran away he left them alone, or when he struck them he left them alone, and those whom he conquered he allowed to herd where they liked, he did not say, 'This is for the chief herdboy.' When they opened up a land for grazing, he took his cattle there, and if he opened up a land, he allowed them to come too. There was nothing like this – 'Stop your cattle, stop your cattle, boy!' At the drinking place they watered the cattle as they wished, although he had not yet watered. All the boys agreed, even with one voice, that Fekisi was a person different from others, not made like other people; he is good, he is kind, he is truthful, but he is a strong man and a great warrior when it comes to sticks. This was the life of the herdboys in Basutoland.

When a man's hand itched, and it wanted to strike, he just went down from the village to the grazing grounds. When he got there he said: 'Bend down, boys,' and then they took off their blankets and bent down. Then he stretched himself over them with a stick. Those boys were beaten simply because they were boys, not because they had grazed their cattle in crops or spare grass. Sometimes two or three men would come on the same day and each one of them would strike as his heart wished. If he were a merciful man, he would say, when he came to them, 'The lark is dead, boys.' When they say, 'It has no presents given to it,' then he is merciful to them, and spares them. But many times the cruel ones say, as soon as they arrive, 'Bend down, boys,' and then the stick sounds. The most painful part is that when the men beat them in this way sometimes the chief herdboys have already beaten them much. Even if a boy goes home in the evening with wounds on him, there is no case made about it.[4]

All these things which we have just spoken of were very painful to Fekisi. He was unable to remain silent when he saw some boys beat others. He felt that if he did not help the one who was being beaten it was the same as if he were the beater. For that reason he always went into the fights of other boys. When he found herdboys fighting, he enquired from others the reasons for the fight, and then he helped the one who was not to blame and the weak. But when he found that the weak one was the one to blame, he would wait a short time, and then go in between them to stop them. He would say, 'Oho! So-and-So, So-and-So has wronged you indeed, but you have beaten him, it is enough. Do not overdo the punishment, or perhaps you find yourself with his fault on your shoulders.'

Such loving deeds of Fekisi and the sympathy he felt for others captured the hearts of all the herdboys of his village. They liked to graze where Fekisi grazed, to herd their cattle where he herded, to water where he watered because there was no one who could withstand him. It was so, it was true. A saying has it, 'My stick strikes, it kills. My shield guards, there is nothing which pierces it. My assegai stabs, it kills because my heart is pure.'

The tobacco, or the bread or the meat which it was said should be shared with the chief herdboy, Fekisi refused. The herdboys of his village did not love him for no reason; he came

---

[4] The wound is considered to be one given in play and not an assault.

to their rescue in many painful matters. When he began to get strong and to feel he was a young man, Fekisi refused to bend down when the men told him to do so. Or when the men said they would make the other herdboys bend, even this Fekisi refused to allow. He said he did not understand why a person should just be beaten although he had committed no fault: this was a thing which would make him obstinate.

This behaviour annoyed the men. Once they tried to combine against him, but he fought them in a way they did not know. The men who had combined against him would be about ten in number. Five faced him, five were behind him. He refused to give in even then, Fekisi the gallant one. He drove together those in front of him, and when they were close together, he struck one and felled him to the ground. Then with the agility of a leopard he was already on the enemy behind. He burst the eye of a man, and before he could cry, 'Jo! I am dead,' he had already broken the arm of one of those in front. Ao! then they ran away.

As they ran away, he called to them in mercy and goodness to take home those wounded in the eye and the arm. Then he prayed them much to give up ill-treating the herdboys as if they were not human beings. When those men spoke of the swiftness of Fekisi in the fight – how he jumped and hit this one, how he jumped and pushed here and there, you would open your mouth wide. But even they agreed with the herdboys, they said Fekisi is indeed a merciful person, he might well have killed many people. They also admitted that he fought only when he was attacked; and even then when he was victorious, he did not pursue.

Do you think the herdboys would not love him? Yes, in truth, they did love him, they clove to him with all their hearts and they honoured him. All the herdboys stopped bullying each other in the days of Fekisi.

There was one thing which the men of the village and indeed all his companions had observed – Fekisi always spoke the truth. He was just, he was kind, he forgave at once those who had sinned against him when they acknowledged their faults and he hated to see people being persecuted. All the people had noticed that in all respects Fekisi had been created in a somewhat unusual fashion. He was far superior to others; there was something he had which they could not describe. Many people began to respect him and to fear him, so that if they were gossiping, especially about something bad, and saw him they became silent. People swearing at each other stopped their curses in his presence, and other matters of this sort stopped when he was there; they were reserved for when he did not see.

From the time of his boyhood up to his youth those he lived with loved him, trusted him, believed in him.

3

Fekisi Enquires about God

Fekisi was a herdboy, as we have already related. He was a model herdboy. In spring time, when he took out his cattle to graze on the young grass, they were not seen when they left the village or when they returned. When it was still dark, before there was any colour in the sky, when the first birds began to twitter, he got up. He took away the bars of the kraal gate gently; he called to the cattle by name, in a whisper. We say he called them by name because they knew him and obeyed him. He turned them out of the kraal just like calves, and they obeyed him, and followed him everywhere he went. So, as he opened the kraal for them thus to turn them out, up rose the oxen, full-grown oxen with great horns indeed, and the cows, and he placed himself in front of them and they followed him. They knew that he would take them where there was much grass and a place to drink, and they followed him like a child who has placed his trust in his elder, that he will look after his matters for him.

He had not played his lesiba instrument when the cattle went out as it was still early. Again he had not even raised his voice talking to them at that time. When the sun rose on them they were far away, among the pastures where there was dampness and greenness, because August is the month in which cattle and all other animals are lean and thin and tucked up for want of grass and water, and at this time others are so weak they lie down and cannot rise. This is also the season when many cows heavy in calf die from poverty. Even today, this month is very hard on stock. It seems also that in those times August was the coldest month of the year. For we hear it said that is the month of 'Boy, do not cry to go out herding. Your months are still coming, there is still to come July and May.' By this is meant, 'It is August of the cold and dust and wind.'[5]

It was a month of suffering, and exposed all the lazy boys who could not herd, because their stock died. The true herd-boys are seen in that month. They do not say anything about the frost or the dust, but get up early and find the best pasture for their herds.

Furthermore the herdboy too fond of a fire was found out at this time by the burns he received sitting too near the fire. A person had his shin bones well roasted by sitting and warm-ing himself at the fire. Again it was the time when the wild animals, such as the rhebok, blesbok, wildebeest and others became weak and dizzy from want of grass and water. The country was ugly and becoming yellow, the wind blew and there was nothing green.

During that time Fekisi tended well the few cattle he had. There was no cow of his heavy in calf which died of poverty, there was no beast of his unable to rise, or lean, because he did all in his power to look after them and to find pasture for them. In the whole village his were the only ones which looked well, even at such a hard time. They did not look like cattle in spring time. As to their swiftness in racing there is no need for us to say anything, as his always beat the others.

There was something which puzzled Fekisi much, night and day he thought it over, but he could not find the answer.

---

[5] As August is the most difficult of all months for the care of stock, the young men, and not the boys, should herd in that month.

This, indeed, was one of the things which made him leave his country and all his friends. When he was tending his cattle and rain fell, it seemed to him a most wonderful thing. He would gaze up into the sky to try to see where the rain came from. He asked himself what rain was, where it came from. What were the clouds? Where did they come from? By what thing were they held of such strength that they did not fall down upon people? And when it thundered, what was it? And what was the lightning produced by in such great waters? As rain came from the clouds it was clear the clouds were water, and how could lightning, fire, come from water? And what was this rain? After a drought and when rain was falling, the cattle were glad and rejoiced. All animals did, even the very insects were glad and the earth was good to look upon.

Yet what really was rain? It was not a great lake, because if that were so, the water would not fall from it in drops, it would come like a great river. It is not even true that rain is made to fall by the witch doctors. Because seeing how much people hate one another, the rain would fall only for the relatives of the doctors and their friends and their fields. But that is not so. It rains impartially for the bad and the good. It rains equally for a person and for him whom he hates. It makes their crops grow equally. Therefore it is not the doctors who cause it to rain. But what is it then? The rain does not come from the ancestors, because ancestors go on hating each other just as men hate each other. If it did come from the ancestors one of them, the chief of the ancestors, would make the rain fall for his own children only, whereas rain does not fall in that way. It rains over the whole country equally.

One day while Fekisi was still asking himself such questions, there was a terrible flash of lightning, and while they were still frightened the lightning struck near where he was. It killed the son of Phakoane and two cattle. Other people were wounded, but lived. On that same day the clouds were very angry.

Some doctors went and sat outside, intending to drive away the lightning. Just then it struck one of them, and the rest ran away, and as they were still running, it struck another one.

Phakoane had gone to a beer drink. He arrived from there drunk and heard that his son had been taken by the clouds. So he took his stick, saying he would beat his wife; for what was she doing at home, that the clouds should take his son? The people of the village stopped him and he came outside in a drunken rage.

At that time, Fekisi had no longer any control over himself from fright. When it thundered, it was to him as if all the clouds had fallen down covering men and things. He hid his face, he put his head between his knees and he cried bitterly. What made him cry was – what is this which does all these things? What is this lightning which splits rocks and mountains? Where does it come from?

When he got home, he asked many questions as to what the ancestors were, and he was told that the ancestors are those who died and were with God. It was said God is just, He is pure, He rejects all evil things. He wants people who are just. At this Fekisi was confused as to the reason why people who knew that were so evil. But he quickly remembered that a human being is a thing that is more stupid than all other created things. Because, although he knows that a certain thing kills him, he does it, and it kills him indeed. Fekisi understood very well about God and the ancestors. He was particularly glad on the days that followed, when he continued to admire God's works.

He had been herding, it was during September, on a day when it was beginning to get warm. He saw some men going out to sow. He watched them for some days as they went on sowing. He wondered where they got such a great hope that

15

the Kaffir corn would grow. He counted the days, and one day, as he was passing with his cattle, he saw that the Kaffir corn had sprouted and was appearing above the ground. He asked himself what it was that caused the Kaffir corn, the grass, the trees to grow. He cheered himself up by saying it was that very God of whom he had heard tell.

It was during the month of November and the sun was pleasantly warm. Rain had just fallen, and he had taken the cattle to the grazing ground very early before milking. At that season the country was green everywhere, the grass was green and plentiful; there was abundance of water, everywhere streams were heard; the Kaffir corn was coming into leaf, it was already high enough to hide an overturned pot.

He was taking his cattle to the drinking place to drink. Wherever he looked, he found it beautiful, lovely, all growing things had sprouted. It was still early in the morning, the sun rose in a clear sky. As it rose, it warmed the earth, it drove away the darkness, and because it was getting warm he drove the cattle gently to the drinking place. Fekisi's bull bellowed, through plenty. The oxen jumped, the cows jumped, the calves joined in, as they rushed to go to the drinking place. Vainly he beat them, the oxen would not obey, they scattered in all directions. They were those cattle which are called 'cattle frightened by a bird.'[6] We have said, it was during the month of November, rain had fallen, the country was wet, the crops were hurrying to grow and it was very pleasant and warm.

The sun rose and puzzled him, it rose as he looked at it, and it mounted gently as he still gazed at it; he wondered what the sun was. It rose in a clear sky, its rays were very bright, because rain had just fallen, and cleared away the grey dim mists which are often there during the spring. It rose joyful and rejoicing

---

[6] That is, very fat cattle.

and shining, like a traveller who is going where he longs to go, who is hurrying on his road, who is eager to arrive where his heart is. It rose like one who travels singing, wearing a crown of beauty on his head, whose heart is full of pleasant things. It rose like the messenger of a chief, who is travelling with a message which makes him joyful, so that he even runs for the joy which fills his heart; there is nothing which can stop him, nothing which can hinder him on his journey because he is the messenger of a chief, and the messenger of a chief is the chief. So the sun rose, smiling and with a smiling face, it looked like the appearing of one who brought good tidings.

And here Fekisi our young man began to be frightened and to wonder greatly. He asked himself, what is the sun which shines so brightly? By what or by whom is it guided on its journey from the East to the West? What is it held by that it does not fall to the earth? Where does it go and whence does it return and how does it go and rise again in the East? And what is this its heat which causes all vegetation to grow, and makes people and animals live? Because the sun is life itself, rain without the sun does no good; the sun is like the bread which we eat every day and by which we live, the rain is like meat, a thing of occasions only. And its strength, how great it is! Its warmth which gives life, its warmth like that of a sitting hen, when she warms the eggs so that chickens may come forth!

This thing puzzled our young man very much. He could not find any explanation.

Fekisi had been happy, but his happiness turned in the end to sorrow. Shortly before he had seen the country dried up, yellow, dusty, windy and ugly with no grass, no water, no green thing anywhere. Suddenly, because rain had fallen, he found a different country. He saw the crops growing fast, the cattle frolicking, everywhere was heard the whistles of the birds. The skylark was trying his best to mount up to heaven,

17

he was saying so in his song. The ground lark, the Bakbakiri and all the singing birds were not remaining quiet.

Fekisi marvelled at the beauty of the country and at the fullness of the life in it. When the sun rose he looked at it and kept on saying to himself how great the strength of it was. He was still at the drinking place, and still happy, but now his heart was made sad by the beauty of this land of his, and tears fell from his eyes. He asked himself where that God spoken of by his elders lived. If perchance a person calls to him, can he hear? Does he perhaps live at Ntsoanatsatsi,[7] where people say they came from?

As he was vainly turning over these things in his mind wild animals appeared on their way to the drinking place, for there were very many of them in those days. The springbok came forward in leaps, and then walked backwards. It leaped, and then looked at itself attentively. It frisked, it played about, and when it leaped it showed the colour on its belly. Where the leader turned off, there all the springbok turned; when they arrived at that spot they did as the one in front did. They came on playing in this fashion; they came towards him and passed close to where he was sitting, so close that if he had wanted, he could have caught one of them with ease. But his thoughts were not on killing. He wondered what it was that gave animals such joy and happiness. Then came some blesbok, moving swiftly to get to the water. And once when he looked to the East, Fekisi saw long files of animals coming, rejoicing at the spring of water. The land was rejoicing and alive.

---

[7] Ntsoanatsatsi means 'rising of the sun'. Ntsoanatsatsi is the name of a hill situated midway between the towns of Frankfort and Vrede in the Orange Free State, and the neighbourhood takes its name from the hill. According to Mr Ellenberger (*History of the Basuto*, p.18), it is an error to suppose that nearly all the Basuto tribes came from Ntsoanatsatsi. Only a very few of them did, and their ancestors were never more than sojourners there.

When the sun was near midday, he roused the cattle up to go home. They were not feeding any longer, the big horned oxen were standing close to each other with their heads touching. They were only hard horned oxen; they stood round him. He thought he would play his lesiba to make himself forget.

But his heart was meditating on many things. The beauty of the country, the joy of all the animals, the joy of all the vegetation, were heavy on his mind. He wanted light on who it was that made the grass grow in its season. By whom was the sun made to rise every day? By whom was the rain made to fall, and where did it come from? What was the lightning? If these things were done by God, who was said to be very just, where was that God? Did He hear if anyone called? Why was He silent when people hated each other so bitterly, and killed each other for no reason?

He drove on his cattle gently, they went home. They went up a valley quietly, they took the ascent gently, and when they arrived at the top, they refused to graze. Some of them even went on by themselves.

There was one beast among Fekisi's cattle whose lowing was mournful. It was a cow with a white face, with horns pointing backwards, but not a great deal. There was another cow slightly grey on the belly and the dewlap. It had one horn hanging down slightly, but its horns were almost those of a shorthorn in their shortness. These two cows lowed in an astonishing fashion. They replied one to the other like people singing. Always it was the white-faced cow which started low-ing, lowing, lowing, and then the grey one replied. She joined in the singing with wonderful precision.

After they had climbed on top, the white-faced one started. She lowed, she lowed, she belched. But she also appeared surprised, because although Fekisi went on speaking nicely to her as usual, there was something strange about him, his voice was not as it always was – it was weak, trembling and sad. And moreover he was not playing his lesiba as he always did when he went to take the cattle out of the kraal at night.

It went on lowing, it lowed and it lowed and then became quiet. The grey one was not joining in, although it was near to her. They were only separated by some of the oxen which were just behind Fekisi. The white-faced cow was on the right-hand side, the grey one on the left.

Again that poor cow lowed deeply, it lowed and it lowed, it lowed piteously. The men in the village heard it and went and sat in the court near the kraal; they began to praise it. The grey cow began to join in the singing just when the cattle were nearing the village. It joined in after a fashion which frightened even Fekisi, their herd. When it started, it lowed slowly, it lowed, you would say, like a cow that was sick and feeling pain.

Fekisi tried to praise it, and praise it much, but as he also was sad at heart, he was unable to praise it as strongly as usual. The white-faced cow went on lowing many times, it lowed, it lowed, its cry became a moaning which reached the high flat ground and the stony hills, it reached even the village. The oxen were not fighting or bellowing, even they on that day and at that time perceived, you would say, that something distressing had happened to their herdboy. We say so because they pressed round him closely, not one wanting to be far from him. They pressed round him so until he entered the bare space in front of the cattle kraal, that many people did not see him; they saw the cattle only.

When the cattle arrived in the village, just as they stood in the open space in front of the cattle kraal, the grey cow moaned deeply, in a tone subdued and gentle, but clearly audible. She lowed once only and then was silent. The tears were dropping from Fekisi's eyes as he sat down in his usual place. All the men were surprised at the lowing of that cow, and they were quick to notice that Fekisi did not appear to be happy.

After the cattle had rested he called the calves out of the kraal and milked, getting much milk. When he was on his way home he had seen the calves jumping about and playing. He noticed also that their hair was shining, because it had been washed by the rain we have mentioned. Their jumping and playing about again brought back to his mind, we may say increased, his wonder. He wondered all the time he milked. He finished the milking and when the shadows decreased, the cattle went out again. After he had finished kraaling the cattle in the evening, he again asked the men whom he could trust whether they would not explain to him fully about God.

As the people realised that Fekisi was an unusual person, they told him the whole truth as they knew it, they added nothing, they left out nothing, they told him as they knew. They told him the things of long ago, of old time, which they had heard told them. They told him about Kholumolumo.

Long ago, they said, there appeared a marvellous monster, with a long tongue, which ate all the people, which ate all the animals. This monster would pick up a man at a distance or a thing at a distance by means of its long tongue and swallow it. It swallowed people alive, and an ox and any animal the same, all things indeed which walked. It roamed about the earth thus, until it finished human beings and animals. Because of the weight of its belly, it sat down, and gathered in by its tongue only.

When all the people were finished up and the animals likewise, a single pregnant woman escaped and hid herself. She was confined whilst still in hiding and delivered of a male child. That child puzzled his mother much, even when he was still young. He was hardly born before he had teeth.

He quickly asked his mother where the people had gone and his mother told him. Then he fashioned a bow, he fashioned arrows broad like a razor and sharp and said: 'Mother, lead me to that monster, that I may kill it.' His mother refused, but at length her son overcame her and she took him.

When they were still a long way off, Kholumolumo saw them. It stretched out its tongue and tried to lick them up, but the boy stabbed its tongue and cut it; it tried to lick them up, he stabbed its tongue and cut it; it tried to lick them up, the boy stabbed its tongue and cut it; it tried to lick them, he stabbed its tongue and cut it; it tried to lick them up, he stabbed its tongue and cut it, and so he went on cutting it; it grew shorter and shorter, and they came nearer and nearer. Kholumolumo nearly went mad with pain and with desire to swallow a human being. It was in a furious rage, its eyes became red, they were as blood, but the weight of its belly overcame it, it could not stand, it could not fight. The boy kept on coming nearer and nearer, and at length he killed it. And then he took a knife and plunged it into its belly.

The greatness of that monster's belly was more than Basutoland of those times, that is to say, that boy could not see the other side of it. He saw only the side he was on. When he pierced its belly a person screamed from inside and said: 'Do not pierce me, make a hole over there.' When he tried to pierce there, a dog howled; when he wanted to pierce in a different place, an ox bellowed. In the end he just made a tear without listening to the cries of those in the belly. Out came people, cattle, dogs – everything living took the opportunity to come out. Then all the people thanked that boy, and they even made him their chief. But soon jealousy arose among the men who had been saved by the boy, at being governed by a boy, and finally they murdered him. My readers know this fable and its ending. I will not relate too many details.

The men told Fekisi the tale of the boy Sankatana.[8] They told him also that there is a God, although He is far away from people, on account of their disobedience. That is why when a Mosuto is in trouble, he says, 'God help me,' and God indeed will help him. Fekisi asked where God lived. They said they did not know, but it seemed as if he lived on the other side of Ntsoanatsatsi. He asked where then was Ntsoanatsatsi. They said they did not know, people had lost it. All they knew was that it is towards the rising of the sun in a great reed bed in the midst of much water, where a vast spring gushes out, where the sun comes out. On account of that reed bed, when a Mosuto woman had been delivered of a child, reeds were stuck into the thatch of the hut as proof that man came from the reed bed. And on account of that great water the father had water poured on him when a female child was born. Again it is on account of that water that children are told that a child comes from a hole in a river, from a very deep place, from a very great water reach.

Fekisi listened to all these matters with deep attention. At night when people were asleep, he rose up and went to a little hill above the village. He sat there and watched the heavens. He saw stars of many kinds, Sefala-bohoho[9] and others had already set. Others rose at midnight, he watched them as

---

[8] The story of Sankatana. This story is very similar to that of Kholumolumo, but has two versions. In the first the boy, after releasing the people from the monster, allows himself to be taken and killed, his heart escaping and becoming a bird. In the second the boy is the owner of an ox called Tddiphatsoa, endowed with magical powers, which warns him of the plots against his life. This ox is taken by Sankatana's enemies, and after many exhibitions of its magical powers it allows itself to be killed and eaten, and its skin is pegged out to dry. Sankatana taps the skin with his stick and the ox rises up alive. The people, their children and the dogs who have eaten its flesh die. Sankatana and his ox go home, and his mother offers Sankatana bread to eat. The ox warns him not to eat it, as it is poisoned; his father eats it and dies.

[9] The evening star, literally the crust-scraper. Its appearance tells the women it is time to scrape out the pots for the evening meal.

they mounted higher and higher. He saw the Molala[10] turning round gently, until the night waned. As the dawn was coming, he saw stars of different kinds, of great brightness, appear. Among those stars appeared one brilliant white star, which shone exceedingly. It appeared to be moving very swiftly on its path. It was not the first time he had seen it. But on that day its brightness terrified him. He asked himself by whom are those things, those stars held, by whom are they guided? As he was still in his night watch, he was very frightened and startled. He heard in the night a cock crowing. Then he watched closely to find at the appearance of what stars the fowl cried. During the nights following, he observed that the fowl cried always at the same time even when it was dark. Then when dawn came he went back into his hut.

In the morning he went out to herd as usual. The cattle came home with full bellies as always. But Fekisi was very perplexed in his mind. Often the daylight came before he had gone to sleep. His heart was aching, was aching for God. His heart was always wishing for great things night and day.

When he thought upon that drunkenness we have already mentioned, such as that of Phakoane and his friends, and all its bad deeds; when he thought about the feasts at which were born the little Makhokolotsos, when he thought how truth was lacking among people, when he thought how badly people treated each other and how might was right; again when he remembered the fable of the boy and Kholumolumo and how the people had killed their saviour, he decided it would be good for him to depart from a race of such great evil. The thing that most lit the fire in his heart was hearing that God had already stood aloof from mankind on account of their increased wickedness. When he was in the fields Fekisi under-

---

[10] Milky Way.

stood perfectly that all things are held by the strong hand of God. From that moment Fekisi mused about very painful things. His heart was despising the evil of men, that is their deeds.

His heart was athirst to see God. Often he would look at the sun with wonder, whether it was rising or setting. He asked himself when a person is dead, where does he end? He does not become nothing. Human beings would not be created to eat and to drink, and after they are dead just become worms. There is a place where they go after they are dead.

He stayed thus a few days turning over in his mind what he could do. At night it became his custom to look at the cattle over the kraal wall to see if they watched over the night like the fowls. And the cattle knew him in an astonishing fashion.

One day, a very painful thing happened, from which Fekisi felt that he must go, and go he did.

4

Painful Things Happen to Fekisi

There was a feast of the boys being held. The son of the chief was coming out of the circumcision school. This son was the first-born child of the chief, the son of his first wife. He it was who would take the chieftainship and follow his father. It was the feast of the heir. All boys of the same age as the son of the chief had been circumcised with him. Even those a little older, who ought to have been circumcised the previous year, were disinclined to be circumcised from a wish to be circumcised with the eldest son of the chief, that they might be his companions and be called by the name of his circumcision school.

For as the Basutos did not know how to count the years, when a person's age was being given, it was said he was circumcised with So-and-So, or he was born during such a war, and so on. And the circumcision of the son of a chief was a very great event.

A great many boys were circumcised that time, and there was a very great feast when the boys came from the school. There was much food cooked, people cooked for their children coming from the school. Even those whose children had not been circumcised cooked much food, to help the chief and to show their love for the first-born child of the chief. The chief killed many oxen, through love of his son, and the women brewed beer indeed.

The day of their coming out dawned.

Fekisi had gone out with his cattle as usual. When the sun began to rise, and he looked at it, his heart was grieved to think of what would happen on that day of the return home of the boys. Even the previous day, those who came from a distance were continually arriving. And even before sunrise, on all the paths there were already files of people walking, strings of people going to the feast, the young men wearing their festival clothes, and the girls likewise, and the older men and women were equally merry. Everyone was rejoicing and full of joy. The young people said, well! we shall work this; some were going for the meat, others for the drink; some were going to the dance, and others on account of the evil designs of their hearts. Rain had just fallen heavily, the ground was soft and wet. On the previous day there had been a shower, and so there was no dust. It was pleasant altogether, everything was full of life, joy and happiness. It was the day of the feast, the feast of the eldest son of the chief.

The heart of Fekisi in the fields was sore and his spirit was sick. In the midst of such great happiness, he alone was sorrowful, his heart was grieved like a man who is ill. The wicked deeds of the people who had been released by the boy from the belly of Kholumolumo, the story of the boy of Sankatana, and especially the thought that God was standing aloof from mankind on account of their evil deeds, weighed heavily upon his spirit. His heart was meditating, was searching. He was pondering over how the earth might be renewed, so that God might have pity and return to mankind. There in the grazing grounds he still went on herding as usual, but his heart was not with his cattle. He was thinking about other things, not about the cattle, and he was wondering how it came that the animals which had no intelligence kept the commandment of their Creator, while man, who had intelligence, turned away.

Even water, a thing which has neither life nor spirit, continues to run in one direction always. The grass goes on growing at the appointed seasons, the ground continues to bear crops. How did it come that man alone turned from the law of his Creator?

The cattle went home at the proper time and Fekisi went in front of them as usual. But as to these cattle, it was already apparent to any person with an eye that something was the matter with them. The cattle entered the village, he milked them, kraaled them and put up the bars.

At home it was nothing but noises like the buzzing of many bees. At his own home there was no one. All had gone to the feast. There was one old man left in the village, an old man who was too feeble to walk, the man who had related the fable of Kholumolumo and other things to Fekisi. Fekisi went to him to cheer himself up, and to ask for news.

Early, early in the morning, the first people began to arrive. The village where Fekisi's family lived was very near to that of the chief, so near that if a person spoke in a loud voice he could be heard by people at the chief's. The people arrived terribly drunk and fights were frequent. There were many people with ears torn off and arms broken, to say nothing of serious wounds; some fell into ditches and broke their limbs. You saw a man simply stretched on the ground vomiting repeatedly, and others made themselves vomit, so full they were of beer, that they might go on drinking. Oho! the evil of that day.

Others went off to steal during that night, and when the owners of the stock wanted to scold them, on account of their drunkenness they fought them. Others fought and injured each other mortally disputing over girls.

The most painful incident of all was that Sebati, a fine man, full of self-respect, a large cultivator of Kaffir corn, a hardy guardian of his stock, a man who did not go to beer drinks, was found strangled, his corpse lying outside his scherm. There was a faint rumour that it was the chief himself in good sooth who had ordered him to be killed with such cruelty. It was said his fault was that he had refused when the chief wanted to buy ten sheep with a beast. He said a young beast was equal to six. It was also said: 'He is proud, he does not come to the feast of the first-born son of the chief; he is proud of his wealth.' When his murderers were overcome by beer, they confessed, they said: 'If you do such things we shall make you like Sebati. We killed him, we men of the chief; as soon as the chief has spoken, we no longer hold back. We shall make an end of you if you do such things to us.'

Phakoane arrived home – he was even dragged, and his wife arrived after her lord and was cursed by him. It ended by his wife answering him back, and then Phakoane took a battleaxe and hit her on the head. The axe sunk in deeply and refused to be drawn out. The poor woman died then and there. Then Phakoane praised himself in his drunkenness, he said: 'I do not begin with you. I always treat those like you in this way. Now you know.' He kept on saying this, speaking to the corpse. When Fekisi heard, he wanted to stab Phakoane but the people stopped him. When he heard about Sebati he wanted to revenge Sebati on those murderers, but again the people stopped him. They pointed out the danger that would fall on him and his family. Simply from the pity he felt for his father and relations he was persuaded. For his own part he felt it would be a thousand times better if he might but die fighting for justice.

The dawn broke, night did not refuse to go. The sun rose, it rose, it mounted higher. The cattle went out to the grazing grounds. Fekisi was terribly angry. He got up and did not eat through anger. It was the first time anyone had seen him so angry. His anger nearly drove him mad. The cattle went out to graze. It was the month of December and rain had fallen. When the sun rose, mist rose up from the ground, smoke rose everywhere from the ground. The country was of a surpassing beauty.

The animals were playing about, jumping, frisking, playing about, the springbok, the rhebok, the blesbok, the black and the blue wildebeest with the hare. The birds were singing and whistling lustily, the Kaffir corn was in full leaf, of a dark green, the crops were growing with vigour; it was evident it would be a year of plenty. The grass was long and dewy, the flowers were in bloom and smelling sweetly, the cattle lashed themselves with their tails when they tasted the grass, the bulls bellowed, the calves jumped about, they were warm, they felt happy.

All things were rejoicing, were glad and were full of life. Above in the air it smelt pleasantly; above in the air the sun was shining in its full glory and was hanging over the earth in mercy and love; the very herdboys were rejoicing; they had stuffed into their bags the remnants of the feast.

In those days and in that month there was no country among all those which the Creator of all things had made which was more beautiful than Basutoland. From the earth there came the sweet smell of the wetness of rain, from the earth came the sweet smell of the wild flowers, underfoot was the dampness, the foot trod pleasantly; the eye did not tire of admiring the different animals, the ear heard songs of all kinds; the country was full of water, the springs were bubbling everywhere; the little streams were running swiftly, murmuring pleasantly over the beds of sand and stones; the water was clear, the drinking places were full, and only waiting for the cattle, the springs were waiting only for the animals to drink – the grass waited for the cattle and the wild animals. A marvellous beauty indeed.

But Fekisi did not see or hear any of these things; they were seen and heard by others only.

His thoughts were very confused and again he was very angry. That anger of his was seen also by the cattle which he was herding. He was not playing his lesiba, he was not singing, he was not looking anywhere but down on the ground. His face was sullen, evil, threatening, it was not shining with peace, it was looking down on the ground. If a beast but tried to stray he scolded it harshly, his voice was evil and rough; for two days even the cattle had noticed this change.

You will admit that all animals, even the very dogs, quickly see when a man is glad or when he is sad. And his cattle which he had herded lovingly for years, which knew his voice, were quick to observe that he had changed. Whether they said he was ill or grieved, that we do not know; they simply observed his behaviour. In the midst of such great joy and rejoicing, one man there was who was sick – Fekisi. He was affected by something, and he did not know what it was.

A great fire was consuming him inside, it devoured him as a horse is afflicted with bots, it becomes dizzy, it sweats, it runs about, it strikes in all directions. It dashes into a person or a beast or anything it meets with, it sees nothing. It has eyes but it sees nothing with them. And it runs about thus and dies far away, it is made to run by that thing which devours it inside. It is made to run by the pain and where it dies it just falls stretched out. So it was with Fekisi.

A thing he did not know was consuming him, devouring his heart in a most cruel way and making him think of running away, not knowing where he had to go, of running away and leaving this land where evil had increased, where people ate one another like beasts of the earth, where truth was unknown, where sin was life, where to steal was to help oneself, where envy finished mankind, even the chiefs, where drunkenness

31

was food. The thing was consuming him, finishing him, it was as though a great flame of fire was lighted within him so that he wanted to cry like a child. His head was aching terribly, his head was wandering, his eyes were black, he sweated, he breathed with difficulty, it was as though he struggled for breath.

The sun rose. It rose as always, as we have said. It shone brightly as always. And now this youth of ours asked himself terrifying questions. He looked at the sun, he looked long at it, he looked at it fixedly as it mounted gently higher and higher. He said: 'Now truly what is the sun? Where does it come from? Where does it go to? By what or by whom is it held?' Truly it does not come from God. A servant of God will not be glad when evil things are continuously being done under his eyes. In appearance, and by deeds, it is like a servant of the chief. But if indeed it is so, how can it rejoice so much when evil prevails and puts an end to good? If God is just, His servant should be just even as God. He began to be suspicious about the sun; all things were distasteful to him, evil to him.

The sun rose higher and higher, the cattle settled down to graze. As it was approaching midday, a tremendous thing happened which satisfied Fekisi that the sun came from God, that the sun was the servant of God. Suddenly, in the twinkling of an eye, the sun changed, it became red, it became as blood; the brightness of it became red. And then as people looked at it they saw it had no rays. It was as if great drops of blood would fall down. It appeared as if a red thing trickling down like water was going to fall down.

Quickly that redness passed away and disappeared and almost at once the sun turned black, it was as though it disappeared behind something or went out of sight. It became small, it became smaller and smaller, and then it disappeared. A tiny spark it was at the end, and then it disappeared.

Then there was darkness, great darkness, a darkness which was blacker than a wolf's mouth, a darkness such that a man could not see the palm of his hand or his blanket, a darkness greater than that of a man with closed eyes, a black, black darkness. The cattle bellowed, they rushed here and there, they fell. The cattle of Fekisi clustered round him, they did not see him, they could only smell him, they made a little group there. The herdboys ran away; some sat down on the ground as they knew that if they tried to go home they would not reach there, they would get lost. The animals ran about, they collided with people, they did not know where they were going. In the villages a person who was outside and tried to reach his hut ran into rocks; if he tried to grope his way to his hut he collided with another person or a dog or something else. The dogs howled, they howled ominously. Everything was confused and terrifying.

People shivered with fright and even Fekisi was terribly frightened; although he had been sulking and suspicious of the sun, all such doubts had vanished and only fear remained. Everyone felt certain that this was the end, that death had arrived.

Now as they were still in such fear, they heard a noise like that of very strong thunder. The noise they heard appeared to be a long way off, it came on rolling nearer and nearer, it was very loud, it was terrifying. It was as the noise of a thunderbolt when it strikes the earth, it was as the noise of a great rock rolling down a mountain.

The people screamed, they said: 'Jo! We die, we die!' It was as if the sun would fall down upon them. As that dreadful noise came nearer, people heard something like voices of people who speak in great anger. Many people died from fright, they died and were buried. Others became wrong in the head, they went mad. They became mad, hopelessly mad. Fekisi, away in the

33

pasture grounds, remembered in this crisis what the old man had said, that if a person calls to God he will hear him and even help him. At once he stood up, he shouted in a voice loud and clear, he said, 'Oho! God of strength and justice who likes not evilness, help me. Lord, Thou knowest I was not in the murder of Sebati or of Phakoane's wife. I would indeed have avenged their blood had people not stopped me. I am a man who hates all evil things, God, as Thou knowest. Oho! help me in this trouble.' A wonderful prayer!

At once, as he finished to pray thus, he heard a small voice, distinct, pleasant, of the sweetest sound which spoke to him: 'Do not fear, Fekisi, thy God has heard thy prayer. Go and seek for truth until thou findest it. Go and seek for God until thou findest Him. At this moment thou art very far from God. May God be merciful to thee on account of the good thou hast done to people, especially to those persecuted and troubled for no fault of theirs.'

This voice was speaking in a low tone, so low that even Fekisi could hardly hear it, but it was pleasant to a marvellous degree. At once the rays of the sun appeared again, the thunder died away. Quickly the sun appeared and lit up the earth, it shone as ever. As the sun appeared the cattle were seen to be angry and frightened. Those of Fekisi were collected round him because they saw and felt that there was something about him, which was not in other people. Then was there rejoicing on the part of Fekisi when he saw the sun again.

He was especially glad because the sun, the servant of the chief, showed that it did not like evil. He was made glad also by the voice which he had heard. He thought it was the sun itself which was speaking to him. But that voice was so small that he was hardly able to be certain that he had heard it. But quickly the joy of the poor fellow turned again into grief, grief deeper than before. He felt only too well that it was useless for him to stay among people of this sort. Moreover the voice said he was far from God, he must look for Him until he find Him. He felt that if he did not stand up and search where God was, it would be that he was refusing God's orders.

But where to look? Here he could not discover in what direction he should go. This difficulty perplexed him greatly, he was overwhelmed. As to going, he wanted to go; it was a long time now that he had made up his mind to go, but he did not know where to betake himself to.

He moved the cattle on gently as the sun got low and they went home. As they began to take the ascent, the white-faced cow began. She lowed, she bellowed, she moaned. Her lowing was as usual, but its tone was clearer than usual, and she lowed for a long time in the same breath. Her lowing entered the hearts of the men in the village, as they were then sitting in the court near the kraal, to ask the old men whether the sun had behaved thus in their youth. The old men said it was the first time they saw it, but when they were children they heard their fathers' fathers say that when they were children the sun had become dark, but not so dark. There was dusk only, but the stars shone. Also it was as if the thunder had not been there, as they did not hear it spoken of. At this the people said: 'Pee, it is nothing wonderful, since it is a thing which does happen although only seldom!'

When the white-faced cow became silent, the grey cow answered her. She answered in a small, clear and pleasant tone, but very sorrowful. She lowed like a cow whose calf has died. She cried like a person in suffering when he groans. She lowed sweetly but in a low tone. Her cry was very different from her usual one. It was almost like that of the day before yesterday, but it passed it in its sweetness, which reached the heart, in its weakness and in its sorrow. The cattle came to the open space in front of the kraal, they came in this way with no word, no praise, no lesiba from Fekisi, he was absolutely silent.

The oxen and the dry cows crowded round him. Each ox wanted to be very near to him. There was none that fought, none that strayed from the path. All the cattle went in the path, simply following the herdboy.

They arrived and stood in the open space. Fekisi went to his hut to fetch the milking vessel, whereas it was his custom to pass on to the court first and to milk the cows when they had rested. When he went to his hut the cattle turned their heads and watched him. The white-faced cow went on with her lowing, looking towards the chief's. The grey cow answered her, looking at Fekisi, it moaned piteously, the grey cow. And then it went to the scherm of Fekisi's family. And when he came to the kraal it came following him, continually crying and moaning and its cry frightened the people. They began to ask one another what calamity these cattle foreboded. They wanted to say Fekisi was a wizard, but knowing his uprightness, his good deeds, his love towards people, they drove away such thoughts. For all that, they wondered what calamity the cattle foreboded.

Phakoane was one of those who had been greatly frightened by the darkness. He screamed loudly, he threw himself violently down on the ground, he said he had killed his wife for no reason and now she was barring his path. And even when the sun was shining, even then he screamed loudly, he said: 'Joo! Joo! I am undone. I was always beating that poor woman for no fault of hers, and at last I killed her for no reason. Jo! Jo! where shall I go to?' This lament was heard by all the people, even Fekisi heard it when he arrived. That poor man was throwing himself on the ground saying something was eating him. He was sweating dreadfully. At last, people saw the fingers of his hands getting cooked, they oozed like meat which has been roasted; his feet and his heels did the same. You may indeed feel pity for him, that poor man.

At last he died, and his face was dreadful to look at, wrinkled, ruined, evil and black, the face of a murderer. When they wrapped him up and went to bury him, the body opened its mouth, opened its mouth wide and writhed, it was like a person suffering dreadful pain. The bearers threw down the corpse, they ran away, and it was buried on the following day. It was so dreadful that those who buried him did so hastily, then they ran away afraid. As the days multiplied, the murderers of Sebati became likewise.

People went to sleep. Fekisi had not been able to sleep for a long time, it was as though he still saw Sebati where he had been strangled. It was as though he still saw the axe which killed the wife of Phakoane, and when he saw it it was still stuck in her head. It was as though he saw and still heard the happenings of the daytime, the darkness, the thunder. It was as though the voice of Phakoane still sounded in his ears. Above everything else this word – 'Seek God, until thou find Him, at the moment thou art far from Him' – was still continually sounding in his ears. He wished to go but he did not know what direction to take. At midnight he was overcome by sleep and slept. In that sleep he dreamed a dream.

Far away, towards Bochaba-tsatsi[11] he saw Ntsoanatsatsi, but he saw it in the distance, in the dusk. He saw the great reed bed, surrounded by the marsh of many waters; in the midst of that marsh were the reeds growing together thickly; in the midst of the reed bed was a small bare piece of ground; in the midst of this space was a great spring gushing out strongly, bubbling strongly; in the midst of that spring he saw the sun rising and appearing there. And on account of the distance, when it was still on its road to light the earth, he saw another

---

[11] The rising of the sun.

sun appearing in the very same place. He then saw for the first time that there is not one sun, but many. In the midst of that spring, but above it in the air, he saw a wonderful glory, shining, flashing, dazzling; he could not look at it. In the midst of the spring but low down, he saw a glory equal to that above it. On each side of that marsh were trees of fine growth standing in lines with wide branches; near them were others of great beauty, bearing fruits much to be desired, among those trees were beautiful flowers, red, yellow, white, all colours.

As he was admiring, there passed a form like that of a man, surrounded by a transparent mist. He just glanced at that form, he saw that it was surrounded by a mist, the hair of that form swept the ground, he did not see where it ended, but it was very very beautiful. The beauty of the face of that form blinded his eyes, tears fell from his eyes. He covered up his head, and at once he wakened up from his sleep. That form was ascending to the glory above, opposite the spring.

5

Fekisi Leaves His Home

When Fekisi awoke from sleep, he no longer continued to ask questions. He accepted, he believed, he had no doubts, he said now God had shown him where he could look for Him. Towards the East dimly in the far distance was something which he well knew was the very home of God. Far, far away, yes, far away towards the rising of the sun he had seen, but though he had seen it in the distance indistinctly he had seen what he had seen. Although he was dreaming, and saw in a dream only, what he had seen was what his heart was continually desiring. By day he heard with his ears in no dream; he heard a voice which said, 'Seek God, until thou find Him.'

In his difficulty as to where he should look he dreamed a dream, and in that dream he saw Ntsoanatsatsi, he saw a figure, a figure like a man. That man whom he saw in a dream at Ntsoanatsatsi was not like other men, even great chiefs were as dust only beside that figure which he saw. These thoughts satisfied him, they showed him the way he should follow; he was glad, he rejoiced, he was at peace – the way to the East, a pleasant way.

All Basuto of those times and even in these days have a great love for the East. When they lose a person by death and that person is put away in his grave, they place him carefully with his face turned towards the East, so that when the sun rises, it may strike against his brow. Even today this is still done. All animals, early in the morning, graze towards the East, or if they are not feeding they turn towards it.

The grass, and especially the flowers, look to the East when it is early morning, they bow themselves in that direction, and they go on turning as the sun mounts.

All things, even those which do not speak and those which do not live, love the East, and it is plain there is some great and wonderful thing, there in the East. That is the reason why our young friend, when he saw these things we have just related were of the East, went on his way in peace, knowing he was going where all living things desired to go.

As Fekisi was an experienced herdboy, watching his cattle with love, he was in the habit of going to the kraal during the night. He was quick to notice a certain day among the days of spring; afterwards he found that it was in the month of December. The sun would rise and set as in other days, but at night there was something strange about the cattle and other animals. When he went to look at them, sometimes at midnight, he found them lying down and asleep. Suddenly as he stood there, he saw the cattle stand up, all at the same time. They all stood up, they all stopped chewing the cud, they all turned and looked to the East. They looked there with a great longing, they looked there with their nostrils wide spread, as though they smelt something there.

Then he ran, he went to see what the cattle in another kraal were doing. He found they were standing up in the same way, but he just thought they were hearing something unknown. As the years followed each other, he found out and understood that cattle and other animals did this thing once a year, and that in the month of December when it was full moon. He found out also and understood that the night on which the cattle behaved in that way, was the night on which the fowls cried so much and filled the night with noise, especially when they cried the first time. Again on that same night the birds chirp before their time. And again there is no man who will say he saw on that night a wizard, or a ghost or a snake, or anything of that sort. He asked himself what it was the animals heard, what it was they saw there in the East, what kind of night was this in which wizards do not bewitch, and fowls cry louder than usual? He did not know, the poor man, and this was one of those questions which troubled him so greatly since he was a person who liked to find out the reason for this thing and that thing.

That night indeed he dreamed a dream, and in that dream he saw, though he saw indistinctly, but he saw what these things were leading up to. And when he saw his way went towards the East, he was very glad at that.

When he woke, that is to say, when he got up from that sleep, he no longer questioned. He took his loincloths – he wore a fine strong cloth, made of a calf skin – he took his two assegais, his battleaxe, shield, hat and two blankets. One of his sticks was of thorn, the other of wild olive, and the latter he loved dearly. It was straight, with small knobs on it, it was fairly broad at the end, it was not short, it was not long, it was a nice length. When he had taken those two sticks, he did not mark, he killed. With his olivewood stick he did not strike twice at one person; he struck once, and that was sufficient. And when he brandished it, he felt his hand tingle pleasantly. He took the two, to defend himself should he meet with thieves.

He took two little bits of cowhide cut from the forehead to make himself sandals on the road; he took his fire-making sticks, that he might light a fire when needed. He took his knife also, though a knife in those days was a thing like a razor. He took all the small things which he thought he might require on the road, since he saw from his dream that the place he was going to was not near.

When he had finished making his preparations, but in less time than we take writing about them, he went outside. He stood there, quite still. His heart said he should tell his family his plan, but he was afraid they might forbid him and say he was mad. He thought he would tell that old man, his friend. Even then he said there is no knowing, he might perhaps say something, or tell people, and then they would stop him. He went out secretly, no man seeing him, no man knowing his intention and his plan.

Before he left, while he was still standing there wondering what he could do, the grey cow lowed; it lowed softly, softly. When it lowed a second time the white-faced cow lowed with it. They lowed softly, softly, as if they wanted him only to hear. They lowed, they lowed for a long time. As soon as they were quiet, the oxen, the fat cows and all the cattle stood up together and looked at him. His heart failed him, he went to the kraal to greet them and to praise them for the last time. When he came near to the kraal, he found the hard-horned cattle were clashing their horns together. The big oxen were by now excited, it was as if a stick cracked away in the pastures. They smelt him, they smelt him; they came crowding towards where he was. He whispered to them, he praised them one by one. He spoke to the white-faced cow, he said:

> White faced Tsemeli, finest of the herd,
> In the greenness of spring it throws off the herdboys,
> The oxen are casting the long hair of winter.
> Where the grass has been burned graze the cattle,
> And black are the faces and eyes of their herdboys.
> If you should get lost, child of peace!
> What herdboys are those who will find you?
> Sweet-smelling Tsemeli, cow of Rakhatoe.
> When sweet-smelling Tsemeli is perfumed,

She is perfumed by girls in the pastures.
What do the girls do when they cover themselves with
    white clay?
It goes and it goes not, it goes not and goes.
Far away on the high ground, the girls dance and sing,
Here the chief herd cooks the first milk.
Beware boys, take heed that you scratch not,
Lest the milk should be spoiled, and the great one should
    fall.
We, the poor ones, have bitten our fingers,
We have wagered the kids of our goats
When you vanquished the gambler Kholoane.
Kholoane who boasted, those cattle of his
Which are with Tsoanyane and Mochesi
Do not run, but they fly!
And there where you meet with the bones of diviners
The high places of people are silent together.
Tsemeli, with white on your forehead
Whose lowing begins at the sun's going down
And reaches the heart and o'erwhelms it,
Which rings through the village while yet
The cattle are still far away,
Tsemeli, you imitate whom
With your lowing so loud and so long?
What say the men of the chief
At the court when they hear?
They will say: 'Tis not fitting, Tsemeli,
For a cow so to low in a village.
The cow of my father reminds me
Of the days and the cattle of old.
In the enemy's hands were they lost
And no man knows where they are.
Your lowing, Tsemeli, is heard

Is heard by the Zulus afar.

To the grey cow, he said:

Cow of the herdboys, with horns upstanding,
Cow of the spring of 'Malekoatla,
Cow with the dewlap of silver and grey,
Which shines like the shield of the warriors of old!
O black cow, leader of herdboys,
You run not, you trot not,
But filled with high pride you pace by in anger.
Sad cheats are the Sefikeng herdboys
They capture the wagtail I hit,
And with a loud roar falls the rock,
It falls on those Sefikeng herds.
O grey one, blue crane so beloved of the men!
No more drinks the cow of the poor man clear water,
But stands all forlorn in the mud of the marshes.
O mother of beauty, revealer of truth!
O Tsoelia, cow of the chief, with your horns
Downward sweeping, disturb not our rest with your
    lowing
Which causes the tears to spring to men's eyes.
The grey cow, the mother of silence,
Long time is she silent refusing to speak,
Her silence is that of a daughter-in-law
When the mother rebukes her in anger.
Listen, O black Tsoelia, to the singing of clever Tsemeli.
Long did she lead you in singing, answer her now,
Tsoelia is one who won't hurry unduly,
She joins in the singing on nearing her home
And at her singing sit silent the men.
In the forecourts the women stop short in their grinding

And even the praisers stop short in their praises;
At the sound of that wonderful singing,
The song of the God,
The God with the wet nose.

When he had finished praising these he praised them all in a common praise.

But he was praising them thus in a hurry, and in a whisper, so that no one might perchance hear him. And it was as if the cattle knew, they were quite, quite quiet; there was none that poked with its horns, none that chewed the cud, none that looked away from him. The eyes of all were on him, it was as if they knew they were seeing him for the last time.

Swiftly he left those cattle of his, he left the home of his father, he left his father and his mother, his sisters and all the people of the village. He went away treading on tiptoe through the village, he went noiselessly. He went away secretly, not a dog barked, none raised the alarm, all was silent and still.

It was at midnight that he left. When he was outside the village he stopped for a while, his conscience smote him, saying: are you really going? And just then he started off running, that big boy. The bundle of the chief was rather a large one; he started running, his stick carried near his ear; he looked straight in front of him.

He crossed the marsh to the east of the village and found it cool, even cold there, but he just passed on. He did not look at anything, he did not turn his head, he looked just straight in front. There were stars out, some were small, some were great; he just glanced at them. He was only looking in front of him, to the East.

When the path turned, he left it and went straight, looking ever in front, eastwards only. He walked quickly, he walked quickly, he ran like a wild animal because he was not out of breath.

He went on, he went on, he went on, the night waned on him far away, and even then he was not going slowly. The night waned on his feet wet with dew, with his clothes packed up, that big boy. The night waned on him as he was on his way, going where he did not know, he did not know where he was going. The night waned on him walking, looking, looking for righteousness, looking for God. The night waned on him running away, fleeing from that increasing wickedness, fleeing from that land in which there was no right. His heart was searching, was meditating, wishing earnestly for some great thing.

6

Fekisi is Mourned by His Family

The sun rose gently, it rose in a clear sky, a sky clear as crystal. It rose with no wind blowing, everything was pleasantly still, not a branch or a leaf was stirring. When the sun rose it struck Fekisi on the forehead, and he was very glad to see that it did strike him on the forehead, and not on one side, he saw he was indeed on the path. He continued to go on running until midday.

When the sun was high, he felt it burning and sweated freely, but today he did not feel its heat, because his thoughts were fixed on one thing – Ntsoanatsatsi. At midday he rested under a tree in the shade. He sat there for a while, then he put his hand into his pouch, took out some food, ate it, and drank water from a spring; after that he stood up and continued his journey. Now fears began to come upon him that perhaps people, away there at the village, might come after him. Although he left secretly, stealthily, who knows, perchance someone or other had seen him, had seen the path he took, and they would tell his family and the people of the village that he had gone by a certain path. But he comforted himself by the thought that probably they would think he went on a visit, though there again he was not one who was in the habit of paying visits. He thought of many of the things which would be said about him. Some will be glad at his going because they feared him, they could not do as they wished when he was there. Others will think that he was very frightened when the sun was darkened, and now his head is wrong. Others will say he was a madman indeed to leave home, no man knowing where he went, not telling a single person even among his companions. He said – of all these things there is not one which matters.

Anyone who feels so inclined may speak of him as he wishes, he may insult him, he may curse him, it is nothing; or if it is said he is mad, there again it does not matter. He himself knows that he is not mad, that his head is not wrong, but he is just doing what he feels it is his duty for him to do. Talk of any kind whatsoever will not cause him to change his plan, or to turn back and go home. Because what good is it for a person to do what he does not want to do on account of people? What good is it for a man to give up doing what he likes on account of people? That is to take on two appearances like a chameleon. The one appearance is that which a person shows the world, the other is that which is his own, which he knows himself to be. That is to deceive one's neighbours, for they will take him to be what he is not; and also that is to deceive oneself as well. Such a life is bad, because it is to act a lie twice at one time, to deceive others and to deceive oneself. It is best for a man to speak as he feels, let him speak his opinion, as he sees, rather than say something different from fear of people.

'It is better for a man to do what his heart says he should do, what his conscience approves of, rather than that he should not do so from fear of people because that is to pretend to be two persons or many – one person in speech, in deeds, in the eyes of men, a different person in secret, in oneself, in mind and conscience. People may say what they say, that does not matter to me. I ought to live my life as I have been created, not pretend to be what I am not. My heart is searching for righteousness and I will not give up that righteousness because all men hate it. My heart avoids all evil, and I will not fear to say so because of people. I had better die, rather than live my life as other people like, and not as I myself like.' His mind was turning over all these things, and he thought: it is no matter, it were better he be defamed and his name spoiled by leaving his home, than go on living at home, when he wanted to leave.

A small matter which was causing him some pain was the remembrance of his father and all his relations. He felt very sorry about his father, when he thought of the questions the people of the village would ask him, and the things they would say to him. And he felt very sorry about his mother, that poor woman, he was very sad about her.

But he said: 'There is nothing I can do. If I had not left them, I could not have lived as I wished. I should go on seeing and hearing the things I do not want to hear. Moreover the voice said I should look for God, and if I had not left them it would be that I refused the order of the great one in order to be with my elders. If they are righteous people, then indeed they are not lost because I have left them; God who said I must go will see to them, will look after them. Again if they are not righteous as they should be, it is their fault – theirs only – it is not mine. Moreover they will die alone, each on his day, one by one. We certainly shall not be together for always, and if I do not go to look for God, when we meet I may find He is pleased with them, and is angry with me because I did not listen to His order. Again if they do not see things as I see them, it is not their fault, it is not my fault, it is how we have been created, that we should not be alike.'

Other thoughts were also passing through his mind. He thought of those cattle, how the poor beasts would be in distress through having no herdboy, not just a herd, but a real herd, a true herd, one herding by love. He remembered their lowing at night when he saw them for the last time. He was indeed astonished when he remembered they acted as if they knew of the plan in his heart. The lowing, so full of sorrow, of those two cows which always bellowed so pleasantly, had changed, was weak, sad and touching the heart. When he remembered how the oxen and the other cattle acted when he left, he felt full of pity for them, and he said in his heart: 'May He who created me thus look after them and look for another herdboy for them.'

Fekisi did not know that at home things were not well with his people.

The sun rose, people got up, and waited for Fekisi to appear, to milk and take out the cattle to graze. They waited, but they did not see him, did not even hear of him. They tried to milk the cows, oh! they refused, they kicked, they ran away. Those two cows of which we have spoken refused even to suckle their calves; their hearts were with their herdboy. Ever since they saw him go, they knew, I believe, that they had seen him for the last time. People were not very much surprised when the cows refused to be milked and kicked them. In those days, even later, I may say even today, it is still so in some places. Cattle know the voice of their herdboy, they recognise him also by smell and they follow him when he calls them. If that herdboy is sick, or anything else happens to him, then there will be no milking because the cows will refuse their milk to any other person, unless perhaps the one who milks them wears a blanket belonging to the herd. That is why when a herdboy goes on a journey, he leaves a blanket behind, so that the cattle may stand still when they get its smell, and allow themselves to be milked. That was so, and is still so in some places even today.

When the people saw the sun getting higher and did not see Fekisi they were greatly astonished, and began to ask questions and to make enquiries.

His father and mother said in their hearts, Our child has been killed by people. They had suspicions against those who killed Sebati, because people stopped Fekisi when he said he was going to avenge the blood of Sebati on those people. People went through the villages to ask who had seen Fekisi, and when the sun declined it found many people in great distress, because Fekisi was much loved of the nation for the sake of his goodness, his love and his defence of the weak. And when the sun struck on the tops of the mountains, the people, especially the women, began to cry; they cried bitterly. The young girls cried bitterly, since there were many among them who waited with great eagerness to be married by Fekisi though he had not let fall even one word. But they all the same had great hopes that perhaps the day on which he would speak would dawn.

There had been much rivalry among the young girls, none wanted to be ignored or unnoticed by that young man, for he was not beautiful in deeds only, he was beautiful in appearance, of a startling beauty. He was tall and straight, he was big, but not thin; he was nicely built, not stout, not thin, he was of good proportions. His face was brown and round, his hair was sleek and not in little tufts, his eyes were black and white as those of a starling, the eyeballs white indeed and glistening, the colour of his eyes was brown, and his eyes were sharp, they were as arrows, but they were kind, they shone with peace always. His teeth were very white, his nose was nicely pointed, but not sharp like that of a white person, his ears feared his hair, they stood out from his head, but they did not project, and they were not too small, his hair was nicely cut and showed his forehead. His voice was deep and pleasant, and when he spoke, it was as if he were singing a song. When he spoke a girl would hang her little head coyly as if she wanted to flirt with him. When he spoke, no one would wish him to be silent.

The mothers of the young girls had looked at him, they hoped for him, they wanted him, it seems, to marry their children. When the girls played or danced or sang, the eyes of all of them were on him, it was he by whom each wished to be noticed. He also it was for whose sake each one sang, they sang for him, although they did not explain it, but each knew this thing in her heart. Twice or thrice some girls who had tried in many ways to bring themselves to our herd's notice were overcome by the love in their hearts and went to the house of his parents. When they came into the scherm they sat about in confusion and there was no lovemaking, though they had come to make love.

The appearance of our hero in all respects spoke for him that he was a 'man'. Meet with him in the path and speak two or three words to him, you feel that you like him, that you trust him, that you are speaking with a 'man'. The whole of his appearance told you that here was a 'man'. Immediately you looked into his eyes, you found they were full of truth, there was no deceit in them. This was why that, when the sun trod the tops of the mountains and people did not see him, lamentation arose. The girls cried for the husband they had hoped for; the women cried for the sake of their children who were bereaved of a true man; the nation wept for their helper who had helped them; his companions went to sleep with sore hearts. His companions whom Fekisi shielded against the chief herds were very sad at heart, they felt that today the shoot of the pumpkin was withered. Some planned to go in search of him, but they did not know where to look for him, since a number thought he had been strangled, strangled because he spoke the truth even in front of the chief, not fearing to say publicly how he knew matters to be. The belief that he had been strangled helped very much to stop people going in all directions to look for him.

52

Where he was, Fekisi was saying that he was being spoken badly of, whereas there was wailing and lamentation for him. The thought that perhaps people would look for him did come to him, but at that he started to run again. He ran all that night, with no rest, with no sleep, he never looked over his shoulder, he simply looked straight in front – Eastwards.

When dawn broke, he had already crossed the borders of the country of the Basuto, he was now in places which he came to for the first time. He went on in this way, running, running, until the sun rose again, but he was not wondering about it so much as usual, the important thing was he felt that now he was where his people would never find him. When the sun rose it rose on strange mountains which he did not know; he only knew that now he was travelling in the country of the Batlokoa. But as to where he was or in what place, he did not know, and he did not like to turn off the path to a village, because by so doing, his people perhaps might find traces of him or at the village he went to he might perchance be recognised by someone who had made the journey to his home in Basutoland, because travelling is unknown, a Mosuto says travelling is a wonder. He decided on that to travel by himself, not leaving the path anywhere.

As he went on walking thus, he was thinking that he was dead to his elders, they would meet no more. He was thinking he was dead to his companions, his friends, his sisters, the village, the cattle, his native land, he was as one already in the grave. As he was still going on thinking these things, he came to a spring – it was the hour when cattle had been grazing for some time – and there he sat down and rested, since he had been travelling for two days and two nights, without sleep, without rest.

7

Fekisi Passes the Country of the Batlokoa

He sat down at the spring and rested there, he drank of its cool water. He took out a little bit of bread and ate, then he lay down near the spring in the shade to rest a while. He drew up his knees, shut his eyes and at once was asleep. He slept a long sleep, a pleasant, refreshing sleep, a sleep which makes one young again and gives one strength. He slept a dreamless sleep.

When he woke he found the sun was already declining, the shadows had lengthened, the cattle would be feeding on their way home. He woke, stood up and looked around, drank some more water, ate and then left; it was pleasantly cool. When he first stood up he felt stiff in his muscles, all his joints felt loose and painful, his limbs were sore; he was like a sick man, his feet had swollen and were painful. He knew well that he was not ill, but it was because he had run two days and two nights without resting, without sleeping, and further he had run among the dewy grass. He comforted himself with the thought that now that he had had a sleep he would recover quickly, and indeed it was so. When he had travelled a short distance he felt his strength come back, the pain ceased and his joints became firm.

When the sun touched the tops of the mountains, he looked back for the first time. Ever since he left he had not looked back, as though if he did so he would see his people coming after him. He turned and looked and then sat down. He saw the mountains of his home, he saw them far away, only their tops were visible. Then he said: 'Greetings, my native land, land desirable among all lands. I would not be here now, were it not for the evil deeds of its people, I was going to live and die in Basutoland. Fare thee well, land of my fathers, where the cattle get fat and the sheep and all animals increase much.'

The tears fell from his eyes, as he saw the sun setting, setting on those mountains of his home. He saw them, saw them far in the distance. Then he said in his heart: 'He who stays behind is he who stays behind. What is liked by one person, another does not like. May those who remain dwell in peace.' He felt that was the last time he would see the mountains of Basutoland.

He stood up and went on after the sun set, he travelled among many villages of the Batlokoa. But he did not turn aside to any, he just passed. When dawn came he was passing a village, there was a great feast on, and dancing, but he did not know what sort of feast it was. As he was going on he came across a drunken man flat on his face on the ground. There were signs that the man had been vomiting a great deal; now he was vomiting blood only. Fekisi stayed there a while, trying what he could to help him.

When the first cocks crew he heard people talking, planning to murder someone. He heard their secret, he heard where it was proposed the man should be decoyed to. Then some went on ahead along the path on which Fekisi was travelling. One returned to the village to fetch him against whom they spoke secretly. They came speaking nicely to each other, in peace, whereas one man had plotted against the other. Fekisi said: 'The behaviour of these men is truly wicked. To speak with a man as a friend when you have plotted to kill him is an evil thing, treachery of the worst sort.'

He stood still and then followed them, treading softly, until they arrived at the place of the murder. They went on walking, and suddenly in the twinkling of an eye four men turned on the one man and struck him to the ground. Before the sticks began to rise, one of them had already fallen to the ground and was screaming. Ere they found out and understood, two of them were on the ground and feeling ill. The remainder ran away, but they ran away wounded. That was Fekisi, he did not pass by any person in distress, he was the helper of the oppressed and robbed.

That poor man who had been helped and rescued by Fekisi thanked him with every kind of thanks, he nearly said indeed he was his God. He asked him many questions, where he came from, where he intended to go and of the manner in which he had helped him. Fekisi answered all these questions shortly. To the first question, he said where he came from, was silent for a short while, and then said where he intended going. His replies astonished his friend greatly.

'You say you come from Basutoland, you left on account of the increasing wickedness there?'

'Yes.'

'You say you are going to Ntsoanatsatsi?'

'Yes.'

'Where is Ntsoanatsatsi?'

'I do not know. I know only that it lies towards the East.'

'What is there, then, that makes you persevere so much?'

'Righteousness, because I search for it. It is where the God whom I search for lives.'

'But, friend, when will you return from there?'

'I shall return no more.'

'When you say so, you mean you will see your father, your mother and your brothers no more on this earth?'

'Yes.'

'You mean you renounce the pleasant things of your country and all the girls of your village?'

'Yes. I have nothing to do with girls. The girls you speak of, it is often on their account that evil happens. Fights arise through these same girls, and murders.'

'There I agree with you. Do you know the reason why those men were killing me?'

'No, I do not know it.'

'I was being killed on account of a girl. I was talking with a fine woman, we understood each other and she became my sweetheart; but afterwards I fell in love with another woman. Now these two women were women those men loved, and when the women threw them over it was said to be for my sake. That is why I say, here I agree with you. But I do not indeed feel I shall ever give them up. The girls over which this quarrel was caused, I shall give them up; but as for others, I do not feel I shall.'

Fekisi was silent for a space, and then said: 'Since now you have almost been killed on account of them, why do you not repent and give them up?'

'No, I was saying I shall –'

Just then they heard a voice of agony, piercing the heart, a voice like that of a man in the throes of death asking for help. Fekisi ran to help, and his friend ran away. Fekisi looked about for a long while but saw nothing, and at last came back to the path and went on. Hardly had he started when he came across a man lying on the ground, dead, but still warm, and plainly only just killed; his brains were protruding. He dragged him to a ditch, and laid lumps of earth over him, so that he should not be eaten by wild beasts. Then he went on his journey, running swiftly to get away from that wicked village.

The night waned and he was already far from it.

On the road many thoughts came to him. It was as if he saw

the corpse of Phakoane's wife, as if he saw the battleaxe stuck fast in her head. It was as if he saw the corpse of Sebati where it was strangled, the voice of Phakoane when he was overcome by remorse rang in his ears; the cry of the man whom he found dead by the path still pierced his heart. All these things grieved his spirit, and then he looked up at the heavens, he looked at the sun, and he found it just the same as always. He remembered the words of his friend, that old man at his village, when he said: 'God has indeed withdrawn Himself far away at the sight of the evil deeds of mankind.'

When that thought came to him, he smelt as it were the evil smell of drunkenness, of murder and such things in the air.

His spirit was disturbed, he breathed with difficulty, and it was as if all the evil things which he saw fouled the earth and even choked him. He remembered the story of the boy of Sankatana, and of Kholumolumo, and he was astonished at the ingratitude of mankind, in being able to plot the death of the person who had rescued them, we may say, who had drawn them out of that grave in which they were buried alive, out of the belly of that monster.

He asked himself what might Kholumolumo be, and did it perhaps make an end of people as evil did, so that there was no man left alive.

Such thoughts came frequently to him on that day. When he rose above them, that is to say, when these thoughts departed from him, he found it was already evening; the sun was already touching the tops of the mountains, night was approaching. Nevertheless he continued to walk until midnight, and then he laid himself under a bush to sleep. He slept well.

When he woke up, he perceived it was already day, and stood up and continued his journey. From the time he left the village of the Batlokoa until the present time he had not seen a village, or a head of cattle, or any other kind of stock, and he did not meet even a single person on the path. It was the last village, not the last of the Basuto only, but the very last of all people. It was the very last towards the East.

From now onwards it was simply desert, a wilderness, where there were no people. It was a country with animals only, a country of great open plains, full of animals of various kinds. There was water in those plains, but not much, and found moreover with difficulty; a person had to know that country well to find water quickly or to know the habits of animals when they went to drink. Where he was was at a very great height on the very tops of the mountains, and he was on the point of descending to come down below to the plains. A person on the tops of those mountains could see far, especially towards the East, because the country fell away, it lay stretched out to the horizon far, far away. Towards the West a person could not see on account of the mountains.

When he had got up he went on walking, going on his journey again. When he was on the edge of the mountains, the sun rose. It rose far, far away, on the other side of all the plains. It rose, shining with peace, shining with love. It rose gloriously, as if it were bringing good tidings. Fekisi looked at it as it rose, and it struck him on the forehead. When it began to rise on him he looked at it steadily, paying no attention to its rays. He found it was a white glittering ball. Its glittering was like a mirror in the sunshine. As he looked at it attentively it appeared to him as if it jumped about. It was as if living things, full of joy and rejoicing, were in it. The sun is like a messenger bringing glad tidings, going along rejoicing with brightness because his message is one of peace, is one of good to all mankind.

As he looked at it, it was really as if he perceived with his eyes the exact spot where the sun came out; not that he saw

Ntsoanatsatsi, but that Ntsoanatsatsi was very near to where he saw the sun rising. Then he covered up his head and said, 'Now what would it be like when he arrived at the place he set out for? Now what would it be like when he arrived at the place he longed for? To the village of the righteous! To the village of peace, of love! At the home of the great chief! At the home of the sun! At the home of all people who had lived uprightly. The home of God himself.

'What will it be like, what will it be like, when I arrive there?'

Then he uncovered his head, looked at the sun very intently and said: 'Oho! God of justice, more just than the sun, shining with a glory brighter than that of the sun, pure, kind, avoiding evil and its taint; Lord, I have left my home to look for Thee. I have heard that long ago in the days of our ancestors Thou didst live with men, but departed from them on account of their evil deeds, Thou didst withdraw Thyself from them. I come to Thee, Lord, I ask for mercy, I ask to be received into Thy village, Lord. I have hated all evil, it is on that account I bring myself to Thee, the righteous one, and I know that I have no claim to be received, because I am a child of those on whose account Thou didst run away. I am flesh of their flesh, bone of their bone, the child of Thine enemies, Lord. But although I am such a one, Lord, truly even I do not like the deeds of my people, they are evil. Oho! have mercy, receive me at Thy village, Lord. Thy word came to me in the pastures, which said, Seek me! and here I am, I have come to seek Thee, Oho! listen to the prayer of Thy servant, and lead me gently on the path until I arrive at Thy village, Lord.'

8

Fekisi Passes through Great Plains

It was an astonishing prayer I have just written; to people of the present time who know a prayer and the way to speak with God, it was indeed astonishing.

It is the prayer of a person speaking with God as though he were speaking to an earthly chief; he makes a request to God in the same way as a man asking for something from his chief. Such a prayer is a real prayer. When a man asks something of a chief, he asks in faith expecting moreover an answer from the chief whom he is asking. And it is right that when a man offers his prayer to God, he should offer it in faith and expectation, expecting what he prayed for to happen, not to make empty words. That is not prayer, that is to play the hypocrite. So when a person asks a chief, he asks him knowing at the time that a chief does not answer quickly; perhaps a man may ask, only to get what he asked after a year has passed or years. Our young friend asked knowing the ways of chiefs, the more so that he imagined God was just a person of flesh and blood like all chiefs; and he asked in the same way as is asked of chiefs. He knew also that chiefs will give quickly to a person only if they are pressed very much. When Fekisi had prayed thus he began to descend the mountain.

He went down with his eyes fast fixed on the East, on the other side of the plains, where he saw the sun rise. On that day there was not even a morsel of bread left, he had not even the smallest bit of dried meat; from the previous day he had slept with an empty belly. He went down and down until he arrived at the foot. He began to descend when the sun rose, it was slanting when he arrived at the foot; it was not that he had travelled slowly, it was from the height of the mountains. When he came to the foot where it was nice and flat, he began to travel swiftly.

He went on walking so, and slept in the open in the middle of those plains. Hunger now overcame him and he slept with his belly crying for food. There were many herds there of animals, such as springboks, blesboks, wildebeest, rheboks, buffalo, hares and many other kinds, and he went to sleep, seeing the animals, but he could not kill them as he had no dog. There was much long rank grass in those plains, and when he went to sleep at night he disappeared into it altogether. He slept in the wilderness far from people, among wild beasts. He heard the jackals howling away on the high flat places, the jackals cried, the spotted hyenas cried and all other things. He slept a very uneasy sleep in that wilderness, expecting the wild beasts to come and tear him in pieces when he had gone to sleep.

He would frequently wake with a start whenever he heard the noise of the wind rustling the grass, then he would spring up thinking, the wild beasts are here. When he was on the point of going to sleep, he would be wakened up by the cry of some animal being seized and devoured by some other animal.

He got up early in the morning before the sun, on account of his fear, and went on his way. He walked with difficulty over these plains on account of the tall grass in them coming above the knees, and in some places reaching to the waist. For all that, he kept going, but he was weak and lacking strength through hunger. He walked in this way until midday, and the sun by now was very hot, so that he was almost unable to endure its heat. The animals vanished; he did not know where they went to. All was quiet and still; the wind was still.

The sun burned on him cruelly and increased his hunger. He sat down fatigued, his eyes bloodshot, his head hanging, his strength gone; hunger was biting him dreadfully. As he was still sitting there, he heard a rustling. He raised his head and saw a springbok coming towards him, and not seeing him on account of the growth. Then he quickly bent down, and before it even saw him he had struck it on the head with a stick and knocked it to the ground. He took out his knife, skinned it and cut away a whole side, then he went to where the grass was not long, made a fire, cooked and ate. For want of water, he drank the blood of that animal he had killed. His thirst subsided, his hunger left him, and strength came back to him.

Then he cooked some meat for the journey and some he cut into thin strips and made into biltong. When he remembered where he came from, he realised that it was very far away. He felt now that he was in the desert, far from any people, in the midst of wild beasts. After he had eaten and made some food for his journey, he stood up and went away.

Before he started, he was filled with regrets and fears; he thought he would return, go back. When he saw everywhere wild beasts only, he was overcome with terrifying thoughts. But as to returning from here he said, no, I had better die here in the wilderness than return. He prayed again to God to help him, to let him pass through all these troubles.

He walked on thus, the sun set, and rose again with him still on that plain. Now he saw the mountains from which he had descended far away, and they had become quite small so far away they were, and it was now high flat plain spread out in front of him. He walked on thus with difficulty for as many days as the fingers on a hand. There was still some meat of the springbok, as he was eating it sparingly, but not much.

But now thirst seized him, his mouth was dry and parched, his spittle dried up, his throat was dry, his eyes were becoming dark. He lifted up his head and saw a hartebeest passing close to him, taking no notice of him. He saw it had nothing to do with other hartebeests, it was going along like a mad animal. It was evident it had run hard, it was tired, its ears were drooping, its tongue hanging out. He followed it, the sun set and night waned. When the sun was high, at the time cattle have grazed well, he saw the hartebeest now walk quickly, hurrying, and bestir itself. Finally it started on a trot. Fekisi, though he was exhausted by thirst, made a fresh effort, and lifting up his eyes saw a clump of trees in the midst of the desert.

When he came to them he found a great spring there gushing out strongly, much water which had even made a marshy place below. It came and drank, that hartebeest. Fekisi came and put down his load, drank and then rested there in the shade of those trees. Now he took out his meat, ate it and was satisfied. He recovered, he regained his strength, his strength came back to him. Then he lay in the shade and prepared himself for sleep. When the hartebeest drank he watched it. It drank, and he thought it would never be satisfied. At last it raised its head, breathed, looked round, pricked its ears and then drank again. After that it came out of the water and lay down by the side of the spring. It came out of that water a living thing, a hartebeest. It came out cunning, swift and covered in mud.

Fekisi was quick to see that the animals would perhaps bother him when they came to drink, as even lions get thirsty. So he climbed up into a tree, I should say into the branches of a tree, and arranged them comfortably, then put his belongings there and sat down. Before he sat down, he turned his eyes on that animal, the hartebeest. He saw that it was now chewing the cud in comfort and was at ease, lying near to the spring. He turned his eyes on the spring and looked at it, and asked himself what the water of the spring was. 'What is this for which that hartebeest leaves the herd, leaves its grazing and travels for days and days continually crying, crying for it? And as soon as he gets it he recovers and lives. What tremendous strength is this that water has? I myself have drunk, and now my eyes are clear, and I am a man.'

While he was musing thus in his heart, he was overcome by a deep sleep.

At midday he was awakened by a great noise. He looked and saw animals of all kinds gathered by the spring. He admired them sitting above them there in the branches of the tree, they not seeing him. When the sun got lower, they left the spring and went to graze. The spring was left by itself. Then he came down, steeped in the water the pieces of skin which he took when he left his home and made himself sandals from them. He also made something like a little leathern bag to hold water when he was travelling. As soon as he finished making these, he ate some more and drank, and then the sun set; once more setting on him in the wilderness.

He climbed back again to the branches which he had arranged for sleeping in. Before he went to sleep he looked at the East, and placed himself before God to guard him in all troubles until he arrived at His village. He expressed his gratitude also that he had been cared for and at last reached this spring. 'I pray Thee Lord God, that oho! Thou takest care of me, look after me on my journey. Feed me when I am hungry, protect me from the wild beasts, fight for me, so that I may finish my journey in peace. Lord, I thank Thee for the water Thou hast given me, I was thirsty, I was tired, I had given up heart. And now I ask for myself, God, from Thee Who art righteous, oho! let me be as these trees in which I sit. Be water to me, refreshing and reviving, that in Thee I may get strong and sink roots deep down.'

When he had so placed himself before God, he slept a long sleep.

9

Fekisi Passes through Dry Places

In these latter days when Fekisi finished his prayer he felt in his heart and had faith that his prayer had been heard. He slept as soon as he finished his prayer.

At midnight he heard the scream of an animal at some distance from the spring. That animal screamed like a dying animal. It was so in truth, a lion was killing a wildebeest. A short time after hearing that scream, he saw two flames of fire coming to the spring, and knew that it was a lion. It came and washed its claws, because it is an animal that takes a pride in itself, the lion. When it had finished it went away to go and eat. He heard a dreadful noise then when it ate, the tearing of flesh, the ripping of muscles, the crushing of bones. This animal eats in a disgusting way. When it eats an animal or a beast, it tears a thigh at once with strength, it takes a large mouthful, it chews but little, it just bolts without chewing. Then it tears off another piece and breaks the bones as it eats.

When it had finished eating, all was still and quiet again. In the early morning, Mphatlalatsane rose, that great star, the morning star. It rose in great brightness, it glittered, it was brilliant. It rose quickly, it made haste in its going. Fekisi looked at it, and he noticed other stars had no brightness compared with it. Then he stood up, placed himself in front of God in prayer and asked oho! that God should not be angry if he continually pestered Him with prayer.

He wished to spend another day or perhaps two at that spring, so that he might rest, but on account of the wild beasts he feared to stay. Before the sun rose, he came down from the tree, filled his leathern bottle with water and prepared to go; he had very little meat left.

He went a short distance and came to the spot where the lion had killed the wildebeest. He saw the lion had eaten and then left it, and was lying down to one side. When he approached, the lion roared in a low tone, but he continued to approach. Then it went away, walking slowly and proudly, going to one side. Fekisi said to himself, whatever happens can just happen. He came up to the wildebeest and cut a piece, he took enough for himself and then passed. When he left, the lion came back, and lay down by that animal. When a person is in trouble, truly God fights for him and cools the anger of wild beasts, even of the lion itself.

That long rank grass was now gradually coming to an end, was becoming less and less and almost disappearing, and there remained grass good for cattle to graze, not thick grass. He walked over those plains for days, he saw no spring, he saw only animals in great numbers; there were jackals, wolves, hyenas. His water was getting low, he was not washing, to eke out his water; though he drank, he drank sparingly. But for all that his water was indeed finished, while he was still in the midst of the desert.

He felt he was just like a person who is lost, far from people, far from villages, alone by himself in the desert among wild beasts, in utter solitude, in silence and stillness. If a grasshopper or any other insect chirped, it struck painfully to his heart, he was startled, he jumped. The cry of an animal frightened him, tore him cruelly; it was as if all these things foreboded some great misfortune which would befall him. The beauty of the country, the beauty of the animals, he no longer saw.

His heart was full of pain, it ached like a headache. He felt afraid, his heart beat fast. It was no longer walking, it was staggering forward. His knees were weak and thin, they were trembling, they could not carry him. Thirst was growing on him, hunger was growing on him. He was dizzy, his eyes were getting dark, were black. He got up with difficulty when he fell down, and after rising he walked on a little, and then fell down again. His back was full of pain, it was as if it were broken. He sat down, and clouds came up.

When the sun was slanting, rain came down heavily and pools of water stood everywhere. Fekisi became wet, but not completely drenched, because an ox-hide blanket, if it is worn with the hair outside, does not let the water through. That rain refreshed him much. It became cool, and the heat and burning of the sun came to an end. He drank the rainwater, fresh water, and then stood up and went on his road, wading through water.

As he went on, he came to a place where a great hailstorm had been. He went on a little and found a dead animal. Whether it was killed by the hail, or killed from some other cause, that he did not know. He took out his knife and cut many small pieces from it. He cut off enough to last him for many days and went on, carrying it. During those days, he walked quickly on account of the coolness and the dampness underfoot and the abundance of water.

When a good many days had passed, and he had continually been walking in this way, he saw far away a black thing making a line which cut across his path, a black line, and he did not see where it ended. He walked on for two full days, seeing this thing all the while, but not coming to it. It was a forest, and as he came nearer to it, it was plainly visible.

One day he came across a lion with a lioness. They say, that animal does not like to be seen when it is with a female. Were a man to see it, the lion would do its utmost to kill him, so that he would never be able to say that he had seen such a thing.

When the lion saw him, it came at him at once. It came at him swiftly, that yellow ox, but God helped him. In vain he glanced hither and thither, he found there was nothing but desert. As the lion came nearer to him, and he had already put his load on the ground, he saw an ant-bear's hole right in front of him. He took up his load and went into that hole. He had barely entered when the lion arrived; it snarled, it roared, it roared. He was unable to go right into the hole on account of its narrowness and he was still close to the entrance of the hole. The lion put in its head to seize him, but it could not reach him. While its head was still there, he stabbed it through the ear with an assegai.

Joo! Joo! Joo! Truly now that lion was almost mad with anger. When it roared Fekisi shook in his very inside. It tried to dig, to dig into the hole, but it soon gave up because it was not made to dig. It drew back its lips. What teeth! What eyes! The lioness also was not quiet. Blood came out, gushed out from the lion's ear. They went away, they disappeared from view.

A short time after he saw them appear, coming swiftly. When they found he was still there, they went back; they did so many times. It was clear he would have to sleep in that ant-bear's hole. They kept on coming during the night, and in the morning they came just as the sun rose.

When they left he came out. Then did he not run! All that day he kept on going with swiftness.

When the sun was throwing long shadows, and he was by now near the forest, his heart told him to look back. While he was looking back, he saw dust rising far behind him, rising up in spurts. He simply saw a thing like a whirlwind advancing swiftly, whereas it was the lion on his trail. The dust rose far behind it. When he noticed it, it was very near to him, with

70

the dust spreading behind it, its mane bristled, its eyes were flashing, its tail was stuck out stiff behind it; the yellow calf did not run, it just bounded. Fekisi ran away swiftly and looked back; as he looked back the lion was just in the act of springing.

In the flash of an eye, he let fall his load and turned round. As he was beginning to turn round he met the lion in the air, it had sprung with an agility greater than that of a cat; he avoided it by getting out of its path. It struck the ground, and before it had time to spring a second time he cut its nose with his battleaxe, and felled it to the ground, because he cut it as it was rising. The lioness was not remaining quiet, and just as the lion uttered its death cry it arrived.

Fekisi sheltered himself behind the lion. When the lioness came near the lion, he loosed an assegai at it and wounded it in the eye, and the assegai even stuck in it.

Au! Au! Au! truly it did terrible things, it leapt about, it jumped here and there. But the drops of blood blinded its eyes, it jumped about not seeing anything, it collided with the lion, it thought it was a person and dug its claws into it. While its claws were still deep in, Fekisi stabbed it behind the shoulder and it died.

He killed lion and lioness at one time, and began to think how it came about that he killed a lion and a lioness, escaping without the slightest wound – he said – by the strength of God.

'I thank Thee, Lord God, for hearing the prayer of Thy servant when I said, protect me from the claws of wild beasts, feed me when I am hungry. Thou hast indeed protected me, Thou hast fed me with things not killed by this hand of mine. I thank Thee, Lord, indeed I thank Thee. Do not become impatient. Continue to look after me thus, Lord.'

When he finished his prayer, he stood up and went on

walking until he came to the forest. As he walked he pondered over the troubles which had come to him on his path ever since he set forth on his journey, and he said perchance these are small things, the great ones are still to come. He came and rested in the shade of a tree; he poured out water and drank; he took out meat and ate.

Many days had now passed that he was living on meat only. Here in the forest he found fruits of various kinds good to eat, he plucked them and ate. When he was rested he got up and went on. The forest was not very thick at the sides, but in the middle the trees met. He came across herds of elephants, troops of monkeys, but he just passed them by, he had nothing to do with them. He had left behind the lion and lioness, he had not even skinned them. These elephants kept away from him, the monkeys pelted him with fruits when he passed beneath trees in which they sat.

As he was still walking on, he came to a great river, running through the forest. He looked, he looked, he saw where there were tall trees which almost met those on the further bank. He came up to them, but found that he could not reach those on the other side. Then he came down and stripped off his blankets. He sounded with a stick and found the water was not deep. He picked up all his belongings and went into the water.

He went on, he went on, he went on, and when he was in midstream, he stumbled and the water came up to his neck. He recovered and rose.

As he was just drawing one foot out of the water, and the other was still in the water, he saw a crocodile coming swiftly at him, coming with its mouth open. He was already out of the water, and he started to run away.

As he was running thus he stopped suddenly, dead still. He saw the very great length of a snake, a thing with a long, long body. He saw the body, but he did not see its head; it was a spotted thing, of many colours. He stood quite still. A crocodile behind, a snake in front!

As he stood in astonishment, he saw a head very close to him, looking at him, quite still, it had already shot out its forked tongue. He was almost dead with fear, whereas no! it was one of those harmless snakes which have nothing to do with people. Then it turned away from him, and went down to the river, and he began to feel relieved.

He felt now that he was indeed lost, he would die among wild beasts and that soon. He ran on, and came to the other side of the forest; the sun had set by then.

When dawn broke, and it was still early, he went on, and when the sun was high, he was on the outside of the forest and saw a little distance in front a greyish black thing. As he came near to it, he saw it was water. It was water everywhere towards the East. Up or down it was water only, everywhere the eye of man could see it was water.

He stood quite still.

He understood now that here was that sea of which he had heard tell. He saw the waves tossing about, crossing each other, and he was astonished.

The thing now was to find a path. Where would he walk to go to the East ?

73

10

Fekisi Crosses the Sea

He slept at that place, and during the night he dreamed a dream. He heard a small voice, a voice like that of long ago which he had heard at his home the day the sun was darkened, and it said – 'Fekisi, do not lose heart, thou art still on the path. Strive on, thou wilt arrive, it is not far away.'

When he heard that voice, he was very glad and woke out of sleep, and when he woke, he saw something just going out of sight; it disappeared in the sky towards the East far in the middle of the sea, but in the sky. This thing was like that form which he saw in his dream, the form of a man of great beauty and with long hair. He had seen it in a dream while at his home, today he saw it and looked at it, here in the wilderness.

He felt that if he could but find a narrow passage by which to cross this sea, that the land he would come to on the other side would be the land he was seeking. He got up in the middle of the night and went along the shore. When the sun rose and he saw nothing, he turned round and went back along the shore. He went on in this way for some days. As he continued to roam about thus, his food became finished. He came to a place where there were no fruits, no animals, no water, but he persevered. He was walking in a land of sand, the sun burned him cruelly. But he persevered for many days, without food, without water. He could not drink the water of the sea, it was bitter and salt and increased his thirst.

He had become very thin, he was simply bones.

At last he fell sick and was seized with a fever. He was unable to walk. He saw something like a path, which left the sea and went towards the West, and when he came to it he squatted down near to it, sick, weak, tired, hungry, thirsty, livid, and with his feet all blistered, not at all a person. When he wanted to sit down he did not sit, he just fell down, he had a fit, he fainted.

When he recovered, he was aware of three men standing by him. They were people white in colour, with hair like the manes of horses, with grey eyes, speaking a tongue he did not understand.

He nearly screamed, but was quick to observe that they were friendly to him. One of them ran and went to the sea. When he returned he came with something which they gave him to drink, and as soon as he had drunk, they took him, they went with him carrying him. They laid him in a little room on their ship, though Fekisi did not know that it was a ship. From that moment he was very, very ill, and there was little hope that he would recover.

But at last he began to recover, and as the days multiplied, he began to feel strong. They stayed there for the space of a month, and after that time they left and went away. They were people who had been sent by the great chief of the East to get him elephants' tusks.

At the time Fekisi arrived most of the men had gone to hunt elephants, and he was surprised when they came back. They came on to the ship, they brought on with them their goods and those elephants' tusks. As soon as their work was finished, the ship moved, drew away from the shore, and went away.

Fekisi had been put to sleep on fine bedding, he was not allowed to get up, and every care was taken of him.

When the ship moved it frightened him, it was as though

it would turn them over. It leaned over this way, it leaned over that way, it fell forward, it went over backwards, and so on. He was very sick, our chief, but that was a great help, because though he had become very weak, as to recovering, he recovered indeed. When he was very ill, those three men nursed him in turn, night and day. Even when they were on the ship, they took good care of him. He was fed with strengthening food, he was clothed with soft blankets.

When he was quite recovered, his clothes were taken away from him, and he was given others, new and soft. He was dressed in the same clothes as we dress in. His loincloths, his blankets, assegais, battleaxe and other things were put aside with care.

He applied himself to learn their tongue quickly, and by that means knew how to speak to them.

They asked him many questions, as to where he came from and where he was going, and many others of the same sort.

'What tribe are you, friend?' It is they who are asking.

'I am a Mosuto.'

'Where is your home?'

'My home is Basutoland.'

'Where is Basutoland?'

'Basutoland is far away over there, towards the setting of the sun.'

'What were you looking for where we found you?'

'I was travelling, and even now I am on my journey.'

'Where are you going, and why do you travel alone in a country which is full of wild beasts?'

'I travel alone, because my purpose is to seek for something which many people do not understand, and moreover, I was forced away by a thing which many people like. The place I go to is Ntsoanatsatsi, where God lives.'

He began to explain to them about all the happenings at his

home, those evil things which harassed him. He repeated to them the happenings on his journey and the difficulties of it. He told them everything up to the time they found him. Then he said, he knew no more, when he looked he was surprised because when he went to sleep he was alone, but when he woke up he found people there, and they of a foreign race.

He asked in his turn, he said: 'Where do you come from, where are you going?'

'We come from the East, our home. We had come to hunt elephants, we want their tusks.'

When he heard they came from the East, his face brightened; he was exceedingly glad to converse with them. 'The East, eh! If that is so, there is another country beyond the sea and that is where I intended to go. In truth that voice I heard in a dream was speaking the truth, when it said, it was not far off.' This he said in his heart.

'You say you come from the East; is there another country beyond these waters?'

'Yes there is, it is our home. And there are other countries as well as ours.'

'Do you not know another land to the East, in which no evil exists, in which righteousness has made its home, in which God dwells?'

'Among all the lands there is no such land. Moreover God does not live on the earth, he lives on high in the heavens, above the clouds, the stars and the sun. We pray to God while we are on earth, and He hears us. We abide by His laws and His commandment.'

'So God has made laws for you?'

'Yes.'

'What are they?'

'Those which denounce all things evil, which say, we must like and do beautiful and right things only and we must love one another. That is the reason why we took such care of you when we found you because it is the commandment of our God that we help the sick and those in trouble. For had we left you, God would have punished us, because He sees us always, even now He sees us, even now He hears us.'

Fekisi was astonished and stared at them. When they saw how surprised he was, they began to explain to him all about their home. They explained fully all about God.

Fekisi was full of joy when they explained all these things, he felt that most of the things they told him were the very things he was looking for. He asked them questions about their government and their customs, but most of all he asked about things touching the word of God.

They told him kindly, they explained everything to him. On his side he told them all about Basutoland, all about the story of the boy of Sankatana and about Kholumolumo. He told them of that thing his heart was always seeking, to find the great Lord who made heaven and earth, the sun and all things, who made the rain to fall and caused all things to grow. And since all these things are good it is clear that He who made them is all good. Also he wanted to find the God who had been driven away by the deeds of mankind.

They told him that some of his ideas were near the truth, but many were wrong. They told him stories of their own land like those of Sankatana and Kholumolumo. They told him also that in the beginning all men were the children of one man.

That man was created by God, and afterwards when men increased in number, evil appeared, and it went on increasing until wars broke out. That is why people have scattered among the countries. When evil increased, God, being just, tried to punish, but man is a creature which will not hear. In the end He cut Himself off from them and left them, He chose for Himself some who listened to Him, He made laws for them and since then He no more lives among men.

Fekisi was quick to observe that these people knew how to talk to each other although they were not together. One man makes little marks, they will arrive and speak where they go to.

He asked and it was explained to him, and then he was taught to read and write. His heart rejoiced exceedingly, when he found that the things he was seeking existed, and even others which he did not know. He accepted all they told him, he believed them. He saw that these people prayed twice or three times a day, they prayed to that God of theirs. He himself learned to pray, and prayed to God with all his heart, all his soul, all his spirit.

They gave him a book of the laws which had been made for them by their God, and he read them with wonderful zeal. Its contents astonished him greatly. It puzzled him, he was as a man in a dream. He wondered where all these matters would end.

He read the story of the Son of God, and he marvelled at the love of God, His long-suffering heart, His patience and His mercy. He read about the Son of Man from His birth up to His death, and His rising from the dead.

He read the story of the Son of Man with tears, with cries, with a heart full of pain, he was amazed at the acts of mankind. As he went on reading, it was as though he saw that lovely form. That long hair. That face shining with peace and love and truth. Those eyes without deceit, gazing with love, with pity. Those eyes so gentle, showing themselves at once to be so full of truth, and mercy whose depth cannot be measured.

All these thoughts crowded into his mind, as he continued to read about the Son of Man.

They went on so for a long while, more than a month before they reached their home. But these men told him that, although they had carried him off, he should not fear; they had taken him just because he was ill. Now that he was recovered, they would take him with them when they came back, they would return him to his own land, from which they had taken him.

At that he refused, he said, he did not want to go back, he had made up his mind to go in search of righteousness. Then they left him alone, saying he would do as he desired.

The faith of this man astonished them; especially when they realised, they heard, of the darkness and blackness from which he came and how he roamed about the earth, looking in vain for righteousness, looking for God. They marvelled at his wisdom, the depth of his thoughts, when he said: 'Many times I sat down and cried, I asked myself questions which were too hard for me; and when I was unable to answer them and to learn the reason of them I would cry bitterly:

'Who is it who created the earth? Who made the heavens and the stars ? Who made the sun?

'What is the sun held by that it does not fall down on the earth? Where does the rain come from, by whom is it sent?

'After what fashion does the grass grow? Why is it that seed when it is sown first rots and then grows, and that growth which comes from corruption produces a marvel? A grain increases to as many as a thousand grains, without counting the stalk?

'Truly there is some secret which I must seek till I find it. People of such great numbers, and cattle, have not been created only to eat and drink, and then to die. There is something else for which they have been created. Also they do not die, there is some place where they go. Because if when a man dies, it is the end, he is finished, he has become nothing, the seed would not grow when it is in the ground; grass would not grow after it is dried up.

'But as the seed rots, and then grows and bears many seeds, and grass dries up and thereafter grows, it is evident that in the case of man, it is not the end when he is dead, but that it is in that earth where he turns into worms that he grows, to appear in a glory brighter than the first at that place he goes to on the other side of the grave.

'Man has not been created for nothing, he has been created for a reason, and that reason is the thing I am seeking when you see me roaming the earth so by myself, among the wild beasts like a madman; and I will not give up before I find what my heart is always crying for, always seeking, on account of which it is unhappy – righteousness and to find God.'

Matters such as these were too difficult for those men of the East. Often the children of Christians are not surprised at the word of God, they are accustomed to it, they make a prayer simply from force of habit. They pray with their hearts not in the prayer, they say 'Amen' not knowing what they were asking. Whereas a poor man emerging out of darkness, a true sinner, prays with his whole heart, his prayer is that he may be forgiven his great sins.

So it was with Fekisi and the men of the East. They were accustomed to the laws of their Lord, they did what was right simply from fear of authority. Whereas our young friend threw himself into it with the whole of his body, with love, urged on by his heart.

11

Fekisi Comes to Ntsoanatsatsi

The first land at which they touched was an island in the midst of the sea of the East. In this island there were beautiful birds, of many kinds. There were green birds with a long tail like a widow bird, very beautiful in their colours. There were green birds, with grey on the breast, there were peacocks with lovely feathers. There were birds of all kinds, some of them very beautiful; even today they are still there. The birds pleased the eyes of our young friend exceedingly. He looked at them and listened to their sweet notes.

When they went on, they passed by the shores of great, beautiful countries and islands, full of animals and birds which our Mosuto was seeing for the first time.

He was full of amazement when he saw the people of these lands: some were brown, some were yellow, some were white; their hair differed considerably, as well as their customs.

Our young friend began to be astonished at the strength of God, he was amazed to find the great numbers of peoples there were, that is their kinds. He knew only Basuto, Batlokoa, Zulu and Bushmen, that is, the inhabitants of South Africa, and he reckoned that was the tale of all the peoples whom God had created.

His journey revealed many things to him he did not know or had even heard of with his ears; this caused him much astonishment. He was amazed by everything because they were new to him, and a wonder. He was astonished also by the steerers of the ship, how they saw their road by night, and even by day.

One day at dawn, when the sun was rising, a man came to where our friend was and said: 'Our country is in sight.' He saw a beautiful land, beautiful indeed. When they came to the harbour, where the ship stopped, they landed, to go to their homes. They were puzzled as to what they should do with him, but they quickly decided it would be best to take him to the priest, that he might teach him thoroughly about God. They took him there indeed, and when Fekisi was presented to the priest, he received him very kindly.

Our young friend asked many questions touching on God, that is to say, touching on his purpose. All his questions were answered, and well answered, the replies satisfied his heart.

The customs of the nation and the life of the country interested him much. The nation was pure, and lived in truth. He felt that this was the very nation among which he could live. We of today would be very surprised if we were to go there, but he was not surprised, because he did not know. His concern was to find purity.

We should be amazed if we found a nation which had no police, no gaol, no taxes and no chief. What did astonish Fekisi a little was to hear it said, there was no chief; God is the Chief; but their acts quickly showed him that indeed it was so. Fekisi learned about God earnestly. He was shown a large and beautiful building, decorated everywhere, where prayers were made to God. The days went by, he was filled with peace, he found the peace of God, he went often to the house of prayer.

A feast was to be held shortly. Before it took place, he asked himself many questions, whether he might not perhaps stay there, although his journey was not yet completed. He prayed that God would show him the road, if his journey was indeed not at an end.

'My God, I ask Thee with great humility to tell me whether my journey is finished or not. As a man I might say, this is the first nation where truth and righteousness are. It knows Thy name, it asks from Thee, and Thou answerest. But I fear to remain without an order from Thee, because when I was in perplexity as to where I should search for Thee, Thou didst reveal to me in a dream what direction I should take. I saw Ntsoanatsatsi, but I do not see it here. That is why I ask that, oho! tell me if I am to go further, because those people say, there is no Ntsoanatsatsi on the earth.'

The day of the feast came, there was no answer, no voice, no dream, there was nothing.

12

Fekisi Comes to the Home of God

This day was the most important of all the days of that nation of the East. It was the great day of the feast, which took place once every year. The nation gathered together from all sides to that ceremony. The house of prayer was great and broad.

The day of the ceremony dawned, it found our young friend waiting for it, and very eager for it. The people went to the house of prayer, and the ceremony began.

The heart of our young friend was not on the earth, it was with his Creator. He thought what it should be like when he finished his journey, when he came to the house of God! What will it be like? How great will be the rejoicing!

The whole nation was united in spirit, it had come with all its heart, it had come before the great One, it had come before the Lord.

The ceremonies of that day began with the sky clear, with no wind, everything pleasantly still.

When the ceremony was half concluded, that is to say, when the sun was slanting, people came in bodies beating their breasts, to pass close to the altar of ransom, where the servants of God were fulfilling their office with reverence. The first body came, and passed after receiving God's blessing. For a space there was silence, as was fitting, each man in that time placing himself before God in prayer, laying bare his heart to Him. At length the high priest rang a bell, and that body returned to their seats.

When the high priest was preparing to sound the bell, he cast his eyes on that first body which had fallen on their knees by the altar of ransom. He cast his eyes over the whole congregation, he saw they had fallen on their knees, and covered their faces. The high priest's eyes met those of Fekisi, and he saw he was also kneeling but was gazing fixedly at the wall to the east of the building above the altar of ransom, he was gazing with exceeding longing, his hands were clasped and held against his breast.

The priest sounded the bell. The first body stood up, and then another priest lifted his voice and read out a sentence: 'You have not come to a mountain which can be touched with hands, nor to a fire which burns, nor to a black cloud – but you have come to Mount Zion, the home of the living God.'

When the priest thus spake, Fekisi rose hurriedly in his seat, and took two steps forward. His eyes were bright and piercing, he was gazing above the altar with all his might, he was as a man who sees a vision, as a man who sees some wonder.

The whole congregation was still, quite still; the priests were still, quite still. Fear and trembling fell upon them. The voice of the priest was still ringing in their ears. 'You have not come to a mountain which may be touched with hands ... but you have come to Mount Zion, the home of the living God.'

When they cast their eyes on Fekisi, they perceived his face was changed, it was bright exceedingly, it shone with a glory, it was as the face of a child newly born.

At this moment there descended from the roof, slowly but steadily as it were a cloud, transparent and white, a mist, plain in the sight of all in the building, which went down the wall, on which the eyes of Fekisi were fixed, and rested on the altar of ransom. Slowly the mist became denser, until it became very dense; the priests fled, they came to where the congregation was sitting.

Fekisi all this while had been staring as though his eyes would start from his head. His face by now was of an exceeding brightness. He had been gazing at that form of long ago which he saw in a dream while he was still in Basutoland, the form of that man so beautiful, with eyes full of truth, love, mercy, eyes of pity. It was that form which he saw that night, when he slept on the seashore.

Now he did not see that form. He saw the Son of Man in his own person, he saw Him in His glory, he saw Him in the house of God.

His beautiful eyes!

Eyes of love, of mercy!

The Son of Man was standing in the midst of six men, three on the right hand, three on the left hand; those men were shining and lovely, a miracle indeed.

Suddenly, in the twinkling of an eye, Fekisi ran forward with his arms outstretched; he came and threw himself on the altar, saying, 'Ahé! my Jesus, I have longed for Thee, oho! Let me go home with Thee, to the home of God.'

The whole congregation was seized with amazing fear.

Suddenly as he thus spake, speaking thus in the midst of the mist, a gracious voice was heard which said: 'Today shalt thou be with Me in My kingdom. Soon shalt thou enter the holy city. Thou shalt reign with Me, because thou hast not been afraid, and hast left thy country for My sake.'

The congregation covered their heads in fear and trembling.

After that gracious voice had thus spoken there was heard the voices of a multitude saying: 'Throw open wide the doors for him, and let him enter, because it is he who has loved the Son of Man in adversity and in prosperity.'

As the congregation uncovered their heads the priests approached the altar in great fear.

They found Fekisi looking up to heaven, the mist had disappeared, his face was full of joy, rejoicing and peace, the peace of one who has found the Son of Man.

When they looked at him attentively they realised that only his body was there. His spirit had gone to his Creator in glory, his body remained in the house of prayer.

Morija Museum and Archives

Visit the Morija Museum and Archives at Morija in Lesotho, in the west of the country off the Maseru-Mafeteng main road, where the Paris Evangelical Missionary Society established its base in 1883. There much material related to the life and works of Thomas Mofolo, to the traditional Lesotho world and the early days of the printing press is preserved and on display. A walkabout of the village from there includes visiting the Sesuto Book Depot where Mofolo was employed, his Training College and the Leselinyana Newspaper Works. The museum's website is at www.morijafest.com